Colne Spring & Henekey's

Graham Matthews

Glenthorne Publications

2013
Published by
Glenthorne Publications
Glenthorne, 24 Lower Camden, Chislehurst,
Kent BR7 5HX
email: graham_matthews@ntlworld.com

ISBN 978-0-9547250-2-0

Printed and bound in the United Kingdom by

Andus Print
Brighton, East Sussex. Tel: 01273 558880

ACKNOWLEDGMENTS

My thanks to Susan Ruffle for her encouragement to write this story, to Lorraine Jones for yet again typing from illegible manuscript; to Lauren (Leicester University undergraduate) for providing medical information; to my wife Daphne for her enthusiastic assistance and literary guidance; to my brother Nicholas for the German language input; to Jill de Warrenne for her assistance; to Elizabeth Matthews (no relation) for her computer management skills; and to Andrew Gillard for proof preparation.

INTRODUCTION

    This story is based on the lives of Jack and Betty Readman and I have used considerable artistic licence in translating them to the characters of James and Millicent Steadman. I am grateful to Susan Ruffle (née Readman), the youngest child of the Readman family, for providing me with the material for this book, both from her recollection and from documentation she has researched and, more importantly, for her permission to use the material as a basis for this novel.

    The book is dedicated to the men and women who suffered loss and separation during World War II, many of whom were and still are known to me personally.

GFM

Chapter 1

'I will be faithful to thee; aye, I will!'
(Thomas Hardy)

This is a love story, more appropriately a story about love with all its passions, individual needs, betrayal, guilt, regrets, compromise, loyalty, compassion and forgiveness and any other of a myriad of human emotions the reader may care to include, having pondered upon the lives of the people with whom we are about to become acquainted.

In the telling of this story it is not intended to present yet another analysis of the abstract noun 'love'. The Greeks had a word for it, or rather they had several which gave great scope for their ancient philosophers to range through the quagmire of erotic, platonic and spiritual concepts with their diverse subsets.

'Love is a many splendoured thing', as the song goes, and once we have been felled by the virus, we know what we are talking about. Rather like attempting to define God, 'O measureless Might, ineffable love' the well-known hymn tells us, it seems that despite the discourses of the sages, we have thus far to accept that *love* is too great for words.

Human attraction, magnetism, or chemistry, call it what you will, is impossible to comprehend. When observing couples as they stroll hand-in-hand in the shopping mall or along the promenade at Brighton, the thought occurs 'What can they possibly see in each other?' or 'Isn't she petite and cute and he, shall we say, maybe a little on the chubby side.' We are guilty of making a value judgment without regard to all the qualities they see in each other. We cannot plug in to the minds of the respectively petite and overweight couple to download the data defining those qualities which are so evident to each member of the partnership. Their shared experience is known only to them. In chemical terms, there are invisible bonds in the epoxy resins which bind them together. Furthermore, switching to our magnetism metaphor, there is also an electromagnetic induction effect in which each member receives from the other something of the other's personality. That which is induced may be subliminally or consciously received and reflected. In simpler terms, each learns of the other's preferences and aspirations and, so far as possible, adapts accordingly so as to please. Why think about these things? It is to focus our attention to the age-old matter of mutual attraction and love with all its manifestations, at the heart of our story.

Loneliness. There's an emotion to consider. To be parted for a few days from those we love engenders a sense of loss, a sense that we are not where we should be. The temporary dislocation can be borne without too much anguish in the knowledge that the absence will soon be resolved. But what if the separation be long term due to service in the armed forces, imprisonment or, as in the present case these pages will reveal, both situations apply? What strain there must be on both parties to be apart for months or even years.

Unimaginable suffering has been endured by thousands of men and women during times of war. Not unmindful of the tragedy for many families whose loved-ones never came back, here our concern is for the millions who did eventually return home. But to what? Had they already received the 'Dear Johnny' letter whereby they returned heavy-hearted having yearned for so long to resume the closeness of their loving relationship or did they bound up the garden path into the arms of their ever patient soul mate, whose crumpled photo had so frequently been removed from the wallet and gazed at; to carry on with their lives, grateful to have had the good fortune to have survived.

Chapter 2

'We can only hope that it will lead to a really new world of Liberty, Equality and Fraternity.'

(John Edward Readman)

On the 19th April 1941, 2nd Lieutenant James William Steadman MB; LRCP, MRCS, disembarked from a supply ship at the port of Suda situated at the north-western end of the island of Crete and was immediately transferred to the 7th (British) Field Hospital three miles west of Canea (Χανιά).

The hospital had been set up in a large open area close to the coast and comprised at least one two hundred foot long marquee serving as a ward, several huts and dozens of ridge tents, altogether accommodating roughly six hundred beds. Each of the tents was painted with a red cross, and to be certain that the whole site could not be mistaken from the air for a military camp or an ammunition supply base, the staff had pegged out in a clear area away from the tents, a large white canvas sheet measuring about twenty by fifteen feet bearing the famous International Red Cross emblem.

Today, Canea is a pretty town with a quaint harbour alive with sun-tanned tourists milling around the many colourful shops and boutiques found along the quayside. By extreme contrast, Canea in April 1941 was the scene of frantic activity, with the whole area swarming with military personnel bracing themselves for the anticipated German invasion; the first airborne invasion of World War II. The sound of anti-aircraft gunfire rarely abated.

In addition to the Allied troops already stationed on the island, some 25,000 British and Allied troops had arrived as a consequence of the evacuation from Greece. For James, this meant long hours in theatre attending to the men wounded during the battle for Greece as well as many military and civilian casualties due to frequent bombing raids on Crete by the Luftwaffe.

Despite the long hours of hard work in the makeshift tented hospital, James found the occasional moment during a lull in the air raids, to walk down to the coast for a 'bathe in the clearest sea as you could imagine, to drink the native wine which is almost as good as a Benskins Colne Spring* or a Henekey's sherry'. He considered that it was 'great fun' to perform operations by the light of hurricane lamps and to rely on 'dog biscuits and rice' for meals. Such was James's great strength; ever the optimist in any situation.

In the first three weeks of May 1941, the aerial bombardment of Crete increased, which supported the intelligence received that the Germans would shortly be launching a major offensive upon the island. Casualties were arriving in large numbers, many having received injuries during the heavy raids on the airfield in nearby Maleme. In this respect the New Zealanders of the 6th (NZ) Field Ambulance Brigade, stationed in a field close to the hospital, were kept very busy.

Being the eternal optimist is all very well but there comes a point when common sense prevails. James began to wonder if he was likely to survive the invasion soon to take place. Perhaps after all he should write home as had been advised by his commanding officer. He settled down in his tent and wrote first to his sister. He couldn't explain to her the seriousness of the situation he was in due to secrecy restrictions, so he adopted a chirpy style to reassure her. He told her that 'we are in a delightful spot..... with snow-topped

---

* In World War 2, Government regulations restricting the strength of beer forced Benskins to stop brewing their famous strong bottled beer, Colne Spring.

mountains in the distance!'. He felt that he was permitted to include information that 'a fairy ship' arrived through the darkness all lit up and carrying the Red Cross. 'She took away most of our serious cases so that this week, we have not had such a rush', he wrote, 'I like the work tremendously but hate the war which makes it necessary.' Then a letter to his brother-in-law Cecil telling him what a grand time he was having in Crete and that he was looking forward to the privilege of being godfather to his son on his return very soon.

In a more sober frame of mind he wrote the following letter to his faithful wife and companion, Millicent. It was their fourteenth anniversary and, finding no other available writing paper to hand, he wrote the letter on a sheet of Leeds Conservative Club headed and crested paper. He crossed out the club address and added his Middle East Forces (M.E.F.) address.

12th May 1941

Darlingest,

How are you feeling on this, the anniversary of our wedding day?

Although you won't get this probably for another two months, I feel I must write to tell you how very much I am thinking of you, how very much I love you, and how very glad I am for what happened exactly fourteen years ago today.

It's the first time we've been separated on this day – yet, although separated in space, I feel very near to you sometimes. What a little boy I was when we got married! You were much more grown up than I was. I loved you then, as much as it was possible for a little boy to love anyone. In the growing up process,

I did a lot of very silly things & yet, really I loved you all the time, even if I hurt you lots & lots of times. Luckily for me you were terribly strong. And now I'm practically grown up, I love you more than ever. I've a sort of feeling that as we get older, our love will grow & grow & grow. And I know, sweetheart, that there will be no more Harrisons. and Rotary club, and left book clubs, and plans for the reconstruction of the world will take their rightful place in life as it should & must be lived. Even Freemasonry, though it will play a big part in both our lives, will be without detriment to those nearest & dearest to me.

Darling, what a solemn letter this is becoming! And I don't feel in the least bit solemn. I feel very, very happy.

And I'm just longing for the day of our return, when the bombers will have stopped bombing, & the fighters from fighting & this eternal chorus of the guns silenced for ever.

All my love, dearest

Your Jimmy
XXX

James held the letter in both hands and reviewed what he had penned. He sincerely meant every word. Life, he promised, 'would be without detriment to those nearest and dearest to me'. His reference to being a 'little boy' and 'grown up' came from his recollection of Trollope's comment that the idea which women have of men is that they are 'creatures that have to be looked after as grown-up little boys; interesting, piquant, indispensable, but shiftless, headstrong, and at bottom absurd'. He was obviously at a very low ebb in view of the circumstances in which he found himself.

Satisfied as far as he could be with the wording, he folded the letter carefully once and then again, and tucked it into an envelope ready for the morning's post bag. Deep in thought, he changed, wriggled into his sleeping bag and extinguished the hurricane lamp suspended above his camp bed. He said his prayers that night more earnestly than he had ever done before in his life.

Chapter 3

'When the flames and hellish cries,
Fright mine ears, and fright mine eyes,
And all terrors me surprise,
Sweet Spirit, comfort me.'

(Robert Herrick)

A mere eight days after passionately writing his letter expressing his heartfelt love for his wife, all hell broke loose on the island of Crete. The Germans made several bombing raids in preparation for the launch of a massive airborne offensive with ten thousand troops ready to land by glider and parachute. One of the raids was on the hospital which lasted for well over an hour, the red crosses having failed in their intended purpose, and many more casualties were sustained. The steady drone of the German transport planes convinced the staff that it was time to evacuate the hospital entirely; several hundred wounded having already been taken off at Suda.

As the airborne armada approached the region of the coast between Canea and Maleme, James ran to the nearest marquee and called out:

"There's no time to waste. We've received orders to move south. If you can make it, grab your pack and muster at the entrance pronto".

About two dozen men assembled on the road outside the hospital, most of whom were wounded but able to walk. To his surprise the party included two men on stretchers; the able bodied bearers grimly resolved to carry their mates to safety. The men were informed that no transport was available, the only way was to walk south across the country to the port of Agia Roumeli where a hospital ship would be standing by. They agreed it was their best chance to avoid capture and set off on their thirty-mile trek.

Their chosen route took them along the road leading to the village of Galatas situated about three miles from the hospital. They had not walked more than two miles when the already spasmodic anti-aircraft fire intensified into a crescendo, as the German transport planes arrived over the Canea and Maleme area. James turned to see a most extraordinary sight as parachutists spilled from the planes. For a brief moment he watched and, perversely, he regarded the spectacle as being beautiful, as though the god of thunder had blown dandelion seeds across the sky.

As the journey to Agia Roumeli would take several days due to the constant threat of being strafed and to the slowness of the stretcher parties, it was necessary to move at night and rest-up during the day. En route, they passed through olive groves and vineyards, stopping awhile in the villages of Alikianos, Agia and Fournes set in the foothills of the White Mountains. As they went from village to village, kindly local Cretans gave them what they could spare by way of food. From Fournes, the band of weary men walked up the winding road to Lakki and thereafter to Omalos. By the time they reached Xiloskalo, they had ascended over 4,000ft from where they had started.

James, heartened by the progress of his party of courageous men, assured them that they would soon be away from Crete and on their way to Alexandria. They arrived at Samaria Gorge which meant the beginning of the end of their strenuous journey which they would accomplish triumphantly in the failing light. As he led the weary group down through the steep-sided gorge leading to the shore, the bay opened up before them. The sea was a beautiful sight to behold in the twilight with the moonlight reflecting off the crests of the gently rippling waves. They had achieved their goal against all odds.

Apart from a number of fishing boats moored against a jetty, the bay was devoid of shipping, save for one fast-receding hospital ship sailing out of the harbour and bearing on its funnel a well-illuminated Red Cross emblem.

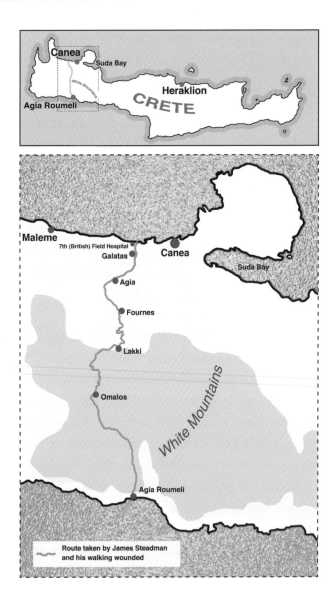

Chapter 4

'Is there no balm in Gilead;
Is there no physician there?'

(Jeremiah 8: 22)

On the 20th September 1936 Dr James Steadman arrived at the surgery feeling pleased with himself for having remembered Millicent's birthday. He was looking forward to the evening after finishing his afternoon round. Sally, his efficient receptionist, had booked a table for two at their favourite restaurant. He nodded to his patients sitting in the waiting room, some thumbing distractedly through old copies of Punch and not really appreciating the humour as their minds were firmly fixed on their aches and pains which, by self-diagnosis, were clearly life-threatening. The occasional cough emphasised the reason for their presence.

Sally greeted him with a deferential smile and handed him the morning post and a pile of files containing patients' notes. He opened each file in turn making a mental note of their extensive histories. They were all regular customers except Mary Bairstow whom he last treated when she was about fourteen years old; a rather skinny creature her overbearing mother had brought in to see him regarding her period pains. Most of the mail was of a routine nature, the month's British Medical Journal, a few consultants' reports and a pharmacopoeia supplement. He flicked through the journal which had articles on the latest advances in the diagnosis and treatment of diphtheria and whooping cough, and a small advertisement on the inside rear cover offering a week's conference for GPs. Having decided that there was nothing deserving of his immediate attention, he got up from behind his desk, glanced in the mirror to check that his tie knot was straight and braced himself for his first patient of the morning.

"Do come in and take a seat, Miss Bairstow," he said a little falteringly as he glanced at this very attractive young woman who entered his surgery. For a moment he stood staring vacantly at the green baize covered sound-proofed door which he closed gently as she assembled herself on the proffered chair. 'Is this the same Mary Bairstow?' he asked himself, 'How the passing of years does change us so'.

He let go of the door handle, assumed a professional air and slid into his swivel armchair. He smiled reassuringly and enquired as to her problem. To his relief the problem did not concern anything of a gynaecological matter as before, but merely a concern for a number of warts which had manifested themselves on various parts of her body. He listened to her attentively, with an occasional nod, as she explained confidentially that she had heard that they 'can turn nasty' and that one may possibly be a naevus and she hoped that she had used the correct term. As he listened, he became distracted and was drifting in his thoughts, mesmerised by her bright blue eyes and all that he could behold from the other side of his desk until suddenly, shocked by his unprofessional thoughts, he brought himself back to the reality that his patient was seeking advice. He dismissed the idea of checking her blood pressure or using his stethoscope to listen to her heart. For heaven's sake man, she has come about some warts!

The other patients were consulted and, being regular attendees, all left thanking their doctor profusely for giving each a remission and a precious document with its hieroglyphic instruction to the chemist. James sat at his desk for a few minutes after the final patient had departed and thought about his years as a GP. He loved his job or rather, his vocation. However, day after day his pattern of life was repetitive; the same patients, the same efficient Sally, the same 'Not to worry' or 'It may be nothing serious but we ought to check just in case' comments uttered with an accompanying reassuring gentle pat on the back.

James idly picked up the Journal and turned to the advertisement on the rear cover. He was about to read the details when he was interrupted by Sally, who reminded the doctor that his afternoon round would involve visits to five patients, one of whom was Mrs Greenhalgh. He sighed when he thought of poor Mrs. Greenhalgh whose life was slowly, but ever so slowly, drawing to its conclusion. She had been dying ever since he first met her four years before. She wasn't really ill but she had reached the age of seventy and had decided that her allotted time of three score years and ten was up and it was therefore time to go.

With a determined effort he stood up, tossed the journal onto the side table and reached for his Gladstone bag. He left the surgery saying goodbye to Sally, who called after him "Do have a lovely evening, Doctor, and give my regards to Mrs Steadman."

He had left the visit to Mrs Greenhalgh until the end of his round. Finding her in a better than usual frame of mind, he felt obliged to spend a little extra time with her, despite feeling all along that he would like to get away as soon as possible. She asked him to convey birthday greetings to Mrs Steadman, he having mentioned the occasion more as an excuse for his departure than to seek her good wishes. After some polite exchange of news about the boys, he took his leave, reassuring her that he would call again at the same time the following week.

The celebratory dinner was amiable but not the most exciting evening of their married life. It was a pleasant enough restaurant, well patronised, and Sally, bless her, had secured a window table with a view of the river. A waiter glided up to the table, took their drinks order with professional politeness, and returned in similar manner three minutes later with two gin and tonics.

After a short time, James asked Milly if she remembered Mrs Greenhalgh.

"Oh yes, I do. She is such a sad person," Milly affirmed.

"Old Mrs Greenhalgh still insists she is dying," said James, "It's quite ridiculous but there's nothing I can do to convince her that she has plenty to look forward to. You know, she has a goodly number of grandchildren who regularly visit her and she is comfortably well off; she pays my fees which is something to be grateful for, I suppose."

They then talked about this and that, particularly about the boys, although his mind was elsewhere. He thought about the possibility of a few days at the Majestic Hotel in early December and was brought back to earth when his wife said:

"Have you chosen what you would like to eat, dear?"

Somehow James succeeded in maintaining interest in the news of church affairs and the boys' school offered by his faithful Milly and the evening passed amicably.

Chapter 5

'Get up, get up, thou leaden man:
Thy tracks to endless joy or paine
Yeelds but the modell of a span:
Yet burns out thy lifes lampe in vaine.'

(Thomas Campion)

The next day, after returning from Lewisham Hospital where he had been operating, James and Milly were at dinner. The meal had arrived on the table at seven o'clock; there was nothing unusual about that as Milly had, without fail, provided his meals at that time for the past nine years: it fitted in with surgery hours. He thanked his wife for what looked rather nice on his plate, improvised a short grace and sighed.

"I hope everything is fine dear," she said intuitively, hoping that it would not be her cooking that was causing his restlessness.

"No, all is well dear, except that I found this afternoon's round a little tiresome." He paused, "By the way, where are the boys?"

"Oh, I sent them off to bed early so that we would be able to enjoy our meal together quietly", she replied.

"That's a pity; I do like to see them for a few minutes before we eat. They are good lads but, oh my, aren't they growing up so quickly. It seems not long since that they used to have the occasional forkful off my plate. I'm pleased to see that they enjoy each other's company. I noticed that they are using their Meccano set we bought them for Christmas; the ship is coming on a treat."

He carried on eating for a while and then stopped, rested his knife and fork on the edge of his plate and wiped his mouth on his linen serviette.

"I'm so grateful to you for agreeing that our family is large enough. As nice as it would have been to have the daughter we had hoped for, I do think it would have made life a little difficult, what with school fees and so forth. These are difficult times, dear, although I'm pleased to note that the economy is steadily improving. Not such good news about Germany's military strength. It is reported that they are now up to parity with us, possibly greater. Winston Churchill is snapping at Baldwin's heels urging the Government to re-arm. It would be terrible if we went to war again."

"God forbid," Milly said, having listened attentively. He was clearly in a maudlin state of mind. She watched him as he picked up his knife and fork as though he was about to continue eating. However, his appetite had failed and, holding the ends of the knife and fork between finger and thumb, he placed them neatly together on the centre of his plate.

"That was lovely, dear, but I've had enough," he said weakly with an apologetic shrug. "I missed the Great War by the skin of my teeth," he continued, "and wouldn't fancy being drawn in to having another go at the Bosch. It is unbelievable that there is a threat of another European war so soon after the recent one."

He paused for a moment and took a deep breath.

"I was thinking, darling," James said, clearing his throat a little nervously as though about to make an outrageous demand. "I was wondering if I could possibly take a few days off. I do need a break and I thought perhaps a week in Harrogate would pep me up a little. I have seen an advertisement in the BMJ which looks just the ticket. It is offered as a revision course for GPs. It's a bit heavy going as some of the papers concern some tricky subjects but I think I would find it awfully interesting. Would you mind staying at home with the children while I'm away darling? I know we usually go together as a family for seaside holidays and bank holiday outings but I do feel that I would be able to concentrate fully on these latest advances without worrying about you and the boys."

All this was delivered rather hurriedly and, as he was composing his speech, he was aware that he should have mentioned the BMJ advertisement earlier, before his plea for a week's break. Furthermore, he was conscious that he had omitted to add that the seminar was to be held in the Majestic Hotel, considered to be 'superior', and that there would be ample opportunity to meet the visiting professors and to socialise with other doctors. The afternoon of the Wednesday was free whereby 'participants may visit the spa or motor through the beautiful surrounding dales' should they so wish.

Milly, having listened to her husband in her usual calm and dutiful way, hesitated before replying. She continued eating and composed her thoughts to reply to his request in a manner which would not offend. She was, after all, a woman of her time; that is to say that, despite the involvement of women for the war effort and their recent emancipation, there still lingered, for the majority of women, save perhaps for ladies such as Amy Johnson and Amelia Earhardt, the notion that they were predominantly home-makers. Nevertheless, Milly accepted that her rôle was to attend to the children and to bring every comfort to her husband in terms of the dinner on the table and, from time to time, comfort between the sheets, though recently this seemed to have lessened somewhat.

She idolised James, whom she acknowledged was idealistic in the love and attention he gave her. At times, she did wonder about extending herself beyond her church interests; she was now a leading light in the young wives group and chairman of the flower committee. She had not continued into further education after she left school which meant that, intellectually, she felt that she did not quite match up to her husband who had so successfully completed his seven years training, had worked up a substantial practice and was in demand as a surgeon. He was highly regarded by his Rotary and Freemason friends; he was a Grand Master of his lodge.

'Jimmy needs some time to himself,' she thought, 'after all he does work so hard, forever looking after other people; added to which any professional development must keep him up to the mark.'

Despite her slight doubts, founded merely upon a feeling of unease at being apart albeit for a few days, she would agree and, furthermore she would positively encourage him to dispel any misgivings he might have.

"Of course dear," she said in the most cheerful tone of voice she could muster, "it would do you good and give you an opportunity to keep up to date with the latest advances. I heard on the radio that a doctor in Chicago had successfully stored human blood for more than a week. What was that all about?"

"Yes, I read about that in the BMJ. I suppose it may be useful, especially if it can be transported. I would imagine it would help casualties in the front line. I pray that we should not be involved in trench warfare once again," James sighed as he dwelt upon the tragedy of the Great War. "I often think about poor Uncle James and the appalling loss of life in Flanders, not to mention the POWs who spent years behind barbed wire."

"So what will you do while I'm away, my dear?" he asked earnestly, for he was concerned that she would not feel neglected on their very first time apart.

"I shall ask Cecil if I could take the boys up to Suffolk instead of staying here. They are old enough to sail with him and he always gets along well with Joseph and Walter. You know how we enjoyed the River Deben last time we were there." Then she added, "We shall miss you, of course, but I know how dedicated you are to your work, my darling, and to have you back refreshed and raring to lead the practice would make us all very happy."

"You're an angel of the first water," he said lovingly as he uttered this sentiment. He leaned across the table towards her, gathered her hands in his and briefly pressed his lips against the tips of her fingers.

"You are so understanding. I'm such a lucky fellow to have you. You're all I ever wanted for my chosen life's companion". She smiled and, slightly nonplussed, returned this unusual show of affection by kissing the top of his head as she did with the boys.

As James sank his head into his pillow that night, following his plea for Harrogate, his thoughts turned to his continuing anxiety. 'What is wrong with me?' he asked himself, 'I can hand out advice and pills to all and sundry except myself! 'Physician heal thyself!' but I have no idea what to prescribe!' Though tired from the stress of the day and incidentally, a large whisky nightcap, he lay awake mulling over his life from school days to medical training and his marriage to Milly.

'She is lovely and so supportive, offering advice when called for. She has become a slave to me and the practice and has provided everything in the house for the boys and me, a true home builder. She's a wonderful cook and I never want for a clean shirt. But I'm bored to death, not with her necessarily, just bored and in need of a change if only briefly. I ought to be satisfied with my lot and just get on with the practice and with any luck I may save a few lives. The boys are great but building ships and cranes with them becomes a little tedious after a while...... We must build that ship big enough for us all so that we can escape from this desert island of tedium; big enough to carry you, dearest, and the boys and Sally and Mrs Greenhalgh and..., and..., the lovely Mary Bairstow with the blue eyes. There's trouble brewing and we must escape from here as soon as we can. We shall need much more Meccano. Ask the boys to run down to the toy shop. We shall cover the holes with olive leaves so that it won't sink and make a sail using my shirts and arm slings from the medical cupboard in the store room. Ropes, we must have ropes. Sash cords will do. Hurry everyone, we must build it as quickly as possible. They are coming to get us. It's our only chance to get away from them. We must escape, we must escape…'

Chapter 6

'Deck the halls with boughs of holly,
Tis the season to be jolly, Fa-la-la.'
(Welsh 16th C?)

The venue for the conference in Harrogate was, as the advertisement had claimed, the prestigious Hotel Majestic; a large Victorian period hotel located near the town centre, yet lying in twelve acres of land and fronted by a well-kept parterre divided by a central path. The hotel had one hundred and fifty bedrooms, some with adjoining bathrooms. James had decided to push the boat out and had instructed Sally to book one of the latter.

On arrival the guests entered through a large revolving glass-panelled door into the reception hall. The hall looked truly magnificent; a thick-piled carpet covered the central portion of the black and white tiled floor and the walls were hung with oil paintings of former mayors and dignitaries of Harrogate. Being Advent, the hall was appropriately decorated with bunches of holly and trails of ivy. A large pleasingly traditional Christmas tree, extending up through the stair-well, was hung with boxes wrapped in different coloured paper and festooned with suitably dignified coloured fairy lights.

'This place is indeed majestic,' said James to himself, as he signed in at the reception desk and collected the key to Room 51, 'I am beginning to enjoy this already'.

"May I carry your cases to your room, sir?" said a hall porter who had been nodded to by the receptionist. "If you would kindly follow me, sir."

James dutifully followed the porter who was smartly dressed in a tightly-fitting blue buttoned suit and wearing a pill-box cap secured by a strap under the chin. They walked past the staircase towards the lift attendant also attired in a smart uniform, this time brown in colour, complementary to the polished mahogany panelled lift cage which slowly ascended to the second floor. His room was located halfway down a carpeted corridor along which they silently strode. The porter, having gestured for the key, opened the door of his room with a flourish and deposited the suitcase and the ever accompanying medical bag on a rack just inside the door.

"Will that be all, sir?" said the porter who was duly thanked along with a florin crushed into the palm of his white-gloved hand. The room was elegantly decorated and everything was found to be to his complete satisfaction. The bed was large but not too soft. He drew aside the net curtain covering the lower half of the sash window and looked out onto the gardens to see one of the gardeners wrapped in a green apron, busily sweeping up the cut pieces of grass where he had been edging the parterre. He was beginning to relax; this was probably what he should have prescribed for himself all along. The conference guests had been asked to gather in the lounge at 3.30-4.00 pm so, having spent time in checking out the place, time pressed a little. He laid out his striped pyjamas on the bed, even though he was unlikely to be needing them as he preferred to sleep without, and put his shirts, which Milly had carefully folded, into the wardrobe.

He soon joined the group of chattering GPs in the lounge who were being handed cups of tea by an attractive waitress, he noted, who wore a black dress with white cuffs and collar and a stiff white linen tiara-like cap. The assembled company fell silent as the President of the General Practice section of the Royal Society of Medicine gave a welcome speech and introduced by name those who were to present papers over the next three days. The welcome speech was followed by polite applause and the general hubbub of people introducing themselves to each other resumed. All looked set for an interesting time. A scan down the list of seventy attendees, which surprisingly included two ladies, confirmed that no other GP came from his area of S.E. London. He was curious about the small female contingent and how they had become doctors, although he was well aware that more and more women were entering the medical profession. He had come across a surgeon active in the North West Kent area but no GPs. His curiosity would soon be satisfied.

Chapter 7

'A dancing shape, an image gay,
To haunt, to startle, and waylay.'

(William Wordsworth)

Dinner having been set for 7pm, James, resplendent in his dinner jacket, new for the occasion, entered the dining room precisely at that time. The room was impressive to say the least, with fluted columns topped with ionic capitals flanking both sides of the hall and ranks of chandeliers depending from the heavily moulded plaster-work ceiling. The seating plan indicated that he would be on Table H in the far corner of the room where he found his place between two men, both a good few years senior to James, who introduced themselves warmly. They soon started chatting about each other's background: James' new companions, who had become friends when they met in the same hospital during the war, sharing their experiences of treating the wounded returning from the trenches.

As James listened intently to his neighbours' wartime shared stories, he could not help noticing a smartly dressed woman, probably in her early thirties, sitting opposite to him. She had been glancing in his direction several times and, during a pause in the conversation, as the two friends made the acquaintance of the diners respectively seated next to them, the woman reached across the table and offered her hand to James.

"I'm Helen Bradbury," she beamed, "so pleased to meet you. Are you here by yourself?"

"James Steadman," he replied and searched for something

sensible to say. "Yes, I managed to persuade myself I needed to keep up-to-date and here I am."

"Who is looking after the practice while you're away, I take it that you do have a practice?" she probed interestedly.

"Oh yes, I do, but I have forced myself to delegate to a trusted locum. I hope he doesn't lose too many of my patients," he joked, not very originally. "Where do you practice?"

"In Totnes, where I live," she replied. "My husband and I have a house on the River Dart, not far from our neighbour Agatha Christie. Have you read her books?"

"No, I'm sorry to say I haven't but I have heard of her, of course," came his apologetic reply.

They chatted on for a while; he talked about setting up his practice in new premises in Penge and she, in turn, explained how different it is being in a rural area with a wide distribution of patients to cover on her rounds and the all too frequent agricultural machine accidents. He suddenly realised that he was forgetting his manners by ignoring his fellow diners and reluctantly disengaged at an appropriate moment. At the conclusion of what was a very pleasant meal, both from the point of view of what was eaten and the accompanying warm conversation with like-minded people, the guests were invited to partake of coffee and drinks in the lounge.

"James, I may call you James, mayn't I? Shall we find a cosy corner to sit; I'd like to hear more about you, especially your involvement with the Rotary and the Freemasons."

James was slightly alarmed at the familiar way she used the word 'cosy', let alone addressing him by his Christian name. Nevertheless, he nodded his approval, though a little apprehensive concerning appearances. Could she be that interested in his social activities?

'She is a very attractive woman,' he thought, 'Oh well, I've come here to relax as well as to recharge, so why not enjoy her company.'

They ambled into the lounge and found a table with two facing leather armchairs. He pulled one away from the table for her. Coffee appeared before them. He offered her the cream jug, turning the handle towards her and, as he did so, he assessed her as discreetly as possible as she stirred her coffee and added sugar, just one lump.

Helen, he observed so far as his expertise in ladies' clothes would allow, wore a dark green *crêpe de chine* cocktail dress cut in fashionable style having a flatteringly fitting bodice with balloon sleeves buttoned tightly at the wrist. A large bow of wide ribbon was attached at the neck, the loose ends of the ribbon lying casually against her bust, tending to draw the eye rather needlessly. The skirt was formed at the front with soft pleats which followed the smooth curves of her body from a waistband down to below her calves. Her shoes were black high-heeled patent-leather button-ups which led his eye to her slim ankles as she sat gracefully with her legs to one side. And what a charming coiffure or hair arrangement, 'whatever one calls it', complementing her oval shaped face.

James, following his general review of her attire, then turned his attention to her face which had been intriguing him since he first sat down at the dinner table. There was no doubt she was a beauty; maybe a little like Vivien Leigh with the same blue-green eyes but these eyes twinkled as did her sparkly drop earrings which had an hypnotic effect on him as they dangled from her earlobes. Again his thoughts were confused as he said to himself, ' 'Thy lips are like a thread of scarlet', when she smiles the sun comes out, she is totally captivating. I know that wine can fuddle the brain but it was only a glass or two.'

He cleared his throat and asked: "So where did you qualify?"

"At the Royal Free," she said. "It all seems some time ago now as I qualified in 1929," she added, anticipating his next question. "There was only one other woman in my group when I was training, so it was nice to be treated as being rather special by all the men there. I had to work hard to be accepted. I think it might have helped that my father is a surgeon. How about you? Where and when did *you* qualify?"

"Me? I was at the Royal London in Whitechapel, a fine teaching hospital if not a very salubrious area. I took a further course in surgery and finished in 1925."

He hesitated for a moment and took the plunge in asking: "I see that you are married, would he be a medical man?"

"Funnily enough, no. Though I did meet my husband Gerald at the Royal Free, but he was a heating engineer, not a plumber you understand, more a specialist in heating installation. He spent several months at the hospital and I gradually came to know him. We married in 1931. Things are fine but he is away quite a bit on business. No children. I say, this is all rather fun pouring out our life stories but I must say it is refreshing having a conversation with you; such a change from hearing the patients' life histories. I take it that you too are married?"

"Yes, does it show?" was his feeble offering in reply. "I have a wife and two boys. They are delightful but mischievous, the boys I mean". He hesitated for a moment: "I am forgetting my manners. Could I offer you a nightcap? What is your favourite medicine?".

"That would be very acceptable. I rather like whisky" she replied, "I hope you don't disapprove".

"Au contraire!", he said as he beckoned to a waiter who, on cue, was passing by their table. He turned to her; "Do you have a favourite malt?"

"I'm rather partial to Glenmorangie, if they have it," she said boldly.

"Of course, madam," said the waiter, flinching slightly to show mock disdain.

"Make that two, please waiter," said James, "and some water".

"Of course sir," came the aloof reply.

They continued their conversation which covered more about their respective practices but also the anticipation of what the next few days of the conference might hold. They listened eagerly to what each had to say, he particularly, snapping up amusing trifles from this delightful new-found companion.

The French ormolu clock on the Adams fireplace gently chimed ten o'clock. James looked at his watch and declared that it was getting towards his bedtime. He stood up and said: "It's been such an enjoyable evening in your company. Perhaps I shall catch up with you tomorrow?"

"I look forward to that. I too must be away to my bedchamber. Goodnight, James." She smiled and stood up offering her neatly manicured hand to shake.

"Goodnight," he replied and gently but firmly accepted her offer.

He escorted her to the lift; James, for the sake of discretion, decided to use the stairs. On reaching the second floor landing, he was just in time to see a dark green clad figure at the far end of the corridor walking in the direction he was about to take. He ducked into an alcove and waited until he heard the door of her room click closed. Peering out to reassure himself all was clear, he quickly found his room, entered, locked the door, put the door key on the desk and flung himself onto the bed.

He lay on his back and covered his face with his hands.

'I am undone!' he said to himself, 'I shall have to avoid her tomorrow at all costs. She is so nice and bubbly and such a pleasant conversationalist. She's so attractive. I'm quite stunned. No, no, this must not be. But I'm curious to know more about her. I feel like one of those wretched sailors being lured onto the rocks. I shall go down to breakfast as late as possible; that way, with any luck, I shall not engage in any intimate conversation with her. I simply can't believe that I could fall for her charms, for that matter fall under the spell of any woman other than Milly. Dear Milly, she is such a sweet creature. How could I possibly feel like this? It's all an illusion. Helen can't be *that* attractive. But she *is*, and I look forward to seeing her at tomorrow's lecture. Perhaps I should concentrate on the lecture. What is it? Oh, no not that, family planning of all subjects! I simply must keep control of myself and not let that lovely creature get to me. I am a respectable married man with a supportive wife and two children. What more could I want? I have not strayed, not at least for a long while and even then it was a mild flirtation which didn't lead to anything. Goodness me, enough breast beating for tonight. Why should I worry, nothing has happened, nothing is going to happen. Enough! I shall have a swig of whisky. That should send me to sleep. Perhaps I'll have a sleeping tablet to make quite sure.'

He heaved himself up and reached for his Gladstone bag. After a swift rummage, he found the bottle of tablets, dispensed one into his hand which he swallowed effortlessly. The unpleasant taste of the tablet was soon overcome by a draught from his hip flask which warmed him as he swallowed.

He slept fitfully, waking on occasions to find himself thinking of Helen.

Chapter 8

It must be understood that in view of James's upbringing, any idea of straying from the path of righteousness was complete anathema to him. His parents were very devoted church-goers and had raised James in all the traditions of the Anglican Church. He was baptised when three months old and attended Sunday School regularly, being confirmed at the age of eleven. During his time at Sunday school he absorbed the stories about Jesus and his parables. He didn't really understand about the woman taken in adultery but he knew she had been sinful and thought Jesus was kind in forgiving her. He remembered his Sunday school classroom and the several framed pictures on the wall. One was a picture of Jesus with long wavy hair under which was the caption:

'Jesus first,
Others next,
Yourself last.'

A second picture was a large print of the 'Light of the World' by Holman Hunt, the original of which, years later, to his pleasant surprise, he discovered in St. Paul's Cathedral. A third picture of his recollection was of Jesus, once more with long wavy hair, standing with his arms around children of all colours and races, under which was the caption:

'Suffer little children to come unto me.'

The fourth picture was called: 'Faithful unto Death' by Edward Poynter, the image of which stayed with him all his life. It was the flaming Vesuvian magma crashing down around the centurion which caught his imagination. The word 'faithful' was to James a goal to which he was determined to strive in all things. Although he wasn't deeply religious, as were his parents, nevertheless he was conscious of a divine presence.

His early education was received in a small Church of England School on the outskirts of Derby from which he obtained a Scholarship to Derby School (later Derby Grammar School), a highly prestigious institution founded A.D. 1160. He took full advantage in his formative years and studied assiduously, gaining his Matriculation at the age of sixteen and, having decided upon medicine, two years later gained his Higher School certificate achieving high marks in mathematics, physics and chemistry.

In the Upper 6th he made friends with a boy named Roger King who, like James, applied himself with enthusiasm to his studies. Roger tended towards the arts and, at the time the two boys became acquainted, he was studying English, History and German. James had been encouraged by the Headmaster to continue French and German languages following his matriculation, particularly German in view of the acknowledged German scientific heritage.

The two friends met up in a small class of students tutored three times each week by Mr Koebel who, though strict, was a kindly man and an excellent teacher. The boys called him 'KK', but not within his hearing of course, after they had discovered that his forename was Kurt. The poor fellow had been interned during the War even though he had lived in England with his English wife for more than ten years and had been teaching here most of that time. He had lost an arm whilst working in a saw mill and intrigued the boys with an account of his grisly accident along with reminiscences of his time in the Isle of Wight internment camp; always in his mother tongue of course. Thus his students were immersed both in formal and colloquial German.

At first James was surprised by Roger's affinity for learning the German language and admired his fluency. The two became KK's favourite pupils and when anyone had produced a particularly good essay, for example, he would allow the successful pupil to enjoy a sniff of the aroma from his tobacco pouch. It wasn't particularly pleasant but this little gesture by their German master to his recognisably maturing boys, contributed in no small part to cementing a lasting friendship.

It was not long into the two boys' relationship that Roger told James about his family background. Roger's surname was originally Koenig, his father having recently changed the name by deed poll to King following the example of the Royal Family in view of the anti-German sentiment among the British people. Now James had the answer to why his friend was so good at speaking German. Although he spoke English at home, he was practically bilingual. 'The blighter, he never let on!' thought James.

As their friendship grew, the two families had become acquainted with each other. James was allowed go with Roger to stay with his grandmother for several weeks during the summer following a busy end of term. She lived in Siegen, a town in Westphalia, surrounded by forests where the two friends enjoyed walking and finding a taste for Hofbräuhaus lager.

With school days over, the two friends promised to keep in touch and meet up during the vacations. James went off to

Manchester University to study medicine and Roger was accepted at Oxford where he read English and History with German as an ancillary subject, finishing three years later to take up his first post as a junior master at Felsted. The promise to keep in touch was not maintained as much as they had intended due to their respective workloads. However, over the next few years they did meet up when they were back in the Derby area visiting their parents.

After three years at Manchester University, where he was awarded a B.Sc. Hons. Degree (1st Class), James was accepted for training at the Royal London Hospital. It was during his penultimate year there that he met his darling Millicent.

Chapter 9

'Cher poison préparé par les anges! Liqueur
Qui me ronge, ô la vie et la mort de mon coeur'

(Charles Baudelaire, The Perfume Flask)

"Good morning, James," said a voice behind him as he was locking the door of his room. Helen, looking cute but business-like in a smart suit, had overslept, possibly due to the whisky night-cap, and consequently was late for breakfast. His escape plan had failed!

"Good morning Helen. Did you sleep well," he enquired.

"Yes thank you. How nice of you to remember my name," she said rather cheekily. ('As if I could forget her name; it's been with me all night,' he groaned inwardly.) "How about you? Did you find the bed comfortable?"

"Yes thanks. I slept like a dog; the best sleep I've had in ages," he lied.

They entered the lift which he had summoned. There were several other guests in the lift which meant that they had to stand close to each other. He felt slightly embarrassed at his intrusion upon her personal space but nonetheless enjoyed the experience, especially as her perfume was stimulating the olfactory area of his brain sending signals to various parts of his body.

"I hope we are not too late for bacon and eggs, I'm feeling quite peckish," said James thinking of something bland to say as they slowly descended.

"I don't usually eat much early in the day; I shall stay with my bowl of cereal and some toast and honey," she said.

In the breakfast room waiters were busily clearing the tables as most of the participants had left.

"Have we missed our chance of breakfast?" said James to an approaching waitress.

"No, sir," the young lady replied looking around the room, "I can re-lay the table for two over there in the bay window if you like, sir, madam. There's a nice view of the garden."

"We would like that," said Helen looking at James for approval. He approved with an "Mmm" and they moved over to the window to admire the recommended view while the waitress removed the used plates, skilfully balancing them along one outstretched arm. The table was soon set and they seated themselves opposite each other smiling warmly, buoyed by the pleasant surroundings. The cereal and cooked breakfast soon arrived and were consumed a little hastily.

"This morning's lecture is of particular interest to me," said Helen after she had finished her toast and honey. "It starts in half an hour so if you would excuse me," she said getting up from the table, "I need to powder my nose," she whispered conspiratorially. He was in the process of swallowing the final mouthful of bacon, so unable to speak, he nodded and gave a little wave with his fingers.

Being a doctor, James was quite used to examining his female patients, of course, but anything which involved contraceptive devices he preferred to refer to the local family planning clinic recently set up in nearby Beckenham. He had half a mind to duck the lecture but his professional approach to everything he did, urged him to attend. Quite possibly there was the added incentive that he would see Helen.

Scanning the packed dining room, which had been temporarily converted into a lecture hall complete with blackboard and easel; she was nowhere to be seen. Neither did he see her at luncheon after the lecture. 'Odd,' he thought, 'I wonder where she is? Maybe it's something I said.' This was a disappointment. He had had two meals in her company and had been looking forward to yet another. 'Ah well!' he shrugged.

The afternoon's lecture on the cardiovascular system and early detection of infarctions was much more of interest to James. The speaker had just started when he turned to see Helen creeping in at the back of the room in a manner which suggested she was invisible. She gave James a reassuring wave which he acknowledged with a smile and a hint of raised eyebrows; he then turned back to face the speaker again, feeling a little more relaxed.

Tea was served immediately after the lecture and Helen and James wove their way towards each other through the buzzing throng of guests.

"I'm *so* sorry," she said, thinking he might be concerned, "I quite forgot to say that I was meeting an old school friend for lunch. She and I were in the same year together. She lives just outside the town in the next village. I knew I was going to be late, we had so much to talk about. Do you think anyone noticed?"

"I don't think so, except for me, of course. I missed you," said James quite relieved that all was well with their recently formed friendship.

"That's very sweet of you," she smiled.

"I didn't see you at the lecture," said James.

"Oh, I sat right at the back near the door so as to make a quick getaway." After a brief pause she said: "Do you think I am being too forward in suggesting dining out this evening? There's a nice Italian restaurant in the middle of town I spotted on my way back. It's near the Spa. What do you think, James?"

"Gosh, that sounds nice," he responded warmly, "I think we shall have had a surfeit of medical matters for one day."

Chapter 10

'But love is blind, and lovers cannot see
The pretty follies that themselves commit;
For if they could, Cupid himself would blush
To see me thus transformed to a boy.'

(William Shakespeare)

It is an extraordinary phenomenon; the numbing of the brain when first one falls in love. All sense is defenestrated. James who, notwithstanding being a studious and generally serious minded fellow, found himself being translated to his youth by a charming sorceress. It was as though he was wearing a magic cloak which made him and his out-of-character behaviour invisible. He became oblivious of the fellow practitioners in the hotel who clearly could not see the expression of bonhomie on his face nor the excess of attention he was paying to his newfound friend.

He enjoyed the grip of her hand around his arm as they snuggled together under his umbrella on their way to the Bella Vista. Such a gentlemanly gesture it is to offer one's umbrella and an arm to hold for security, were her thoughts as they hurried along.

They burst into the entrance of the restaurant, laughing as they did, much relieved to be out of the heavy downpour. The proprietor greeted them in Italian and took their coats and umbrella. Once seated and settled with their aperitifs, the couple fell to chatting eagerly for some time, she telling him about her school friend Anna and he responding in like kind recounting the friendship he had with Roger and his parents.

"Are you ready to order Signora, Signor?" said a beaming waiter whom they had not noticed as he had sidled quietly up to the table. His English was good but heavily accented, which the couple found charming.

"Just let us have another five minutes please, there's so much choice," lied James as though they had even given the menu so much as a glance. He lowered his voice: "I always find choosing from the menu a tricky business. One is either overwhelmed with choice or embarrassed by not liking anything at all. I shall need your help, Helen."

They spent the requested extension of time peering through the menu and using their limited knowledge of Italian to translate the choices on offer. The waiter appeared in timely fashion and stood patiently with pad in hand and pencil poised.

"Waiter, what would you recommend for a fish course?" asked James.

"Ah! Signor, I can recommend *all* our pesce," said the waiter with a twinkle in his eye, "I think you would like the sole, Signor".

James, rising to the levity, asked "Is the sole *Dover* sole?"

"I am not so sure that he comes from Dover exactly, Signor -possibly from Ramsgate!"

This little joke set the mood for the rest of the meal and James found himself loosening up from his usual serious approach to everything in life. He was quite pleased with himself for find-ing another side to his character which had lain dormant for some time. He found the restaurant rather pleasant with its raffia wrapped Chianti bottles hanging from the ceiling and murals of the Leaning Tower and the Amalfi coast adding to the already romantic haze which enveloped him. And what a difference it makes to be greeted so warmly. Is it the Latin effect? Do the French and Italians really love lovers?

With the meal over and the bill settled by James after he had gently insisted against her protestations, the couple exchanged greetings with the proprietor giving him assurance of their satisfaction and promise to return. On stepping out on to the pavement, they were pleased to find that the rain had stopped, which left the pavements glistening as they reflected the light from the street lamps. She held his arm as they walked, no matter that the umbrella had been furled. Everywhere smelled fresh after the rain, which still dripped occasionally from branches overhanging the pavement. James felt very content and, on his enquiring, she too was very content.

Back at the hotel and once again seated in the lounge with their whisky nightcaps; this time Laphroaig by way of daring extravagance, they discussed the following day's choice of a visit to the Harrogate Spa or a coach tour through the famous Yorkshire Dales. They chose the latter and arranged to meet after lunch having agreed that perhaps discretion should prevail; no breakfast or luncheon liaison would be sought by mutual consent.

"Maybe we should be making tracks," suggested James emptying his glass of the last few drops of malt whisky and starting to rise from his seat.

"I quite agree," she replied, "we have another interesting day ahead. I'm very much enjoying this. I really did think that the week would be heavy going having looked through the list of lectures, apart of course from the Wednesday afternoon. I hadn't expected to find someone like you here!"

"Like me, what do you mean?" he replied, a little surprised. He sat down again. "Well," she said "it is not often that I come across a man who is so attentive and caring. I have noticed that you are always on the look out to help. I don't think it is solely due to your profession. Also you are a thoughtful man, clearly dedicated to your calling and quite serious but I suspect there is some trait hiding within you yearning to escape. There, I'm sounding like a psychiatrist. I hope I haven't offended you."

"Not a bit," said James, "I'm rather flattered in one way. Yes, I am fairly serious minded but I do hope not dull. I have to admit that after ten years building up the practice and attending to several thousand patients' ailments and many of their domestic problems, I have tended to retreat in to myself a little. You must find in your practice that the routine does become a little wearing."

"Yes, I do from time to time," she agreed, "but it is all worthwhile when the occasional patient shows appreciation. I wouldn't want any other job."

"Certainly not," he affirmed.

"It's all very interesting, isn't it, what we do with our lives. I hope we shall be able to find time to continue exploring ideas now that we are a little more acquainted."

"I'm sure we shall," he said.

He escorted her to the lift and they both entered.

"Which floor, madam?" asked the liftman.

"Second floor, please," said Helen.

"And you sir?"

"Er, second floor too," said James.

"Oh your room is on the same floor as mine!"

"Yes, so it seems," said James feigning all knowledge of his having discovered this piece of intelligence the night before.

"I'm right along at the far end," she said as they stepped out of the lift. Where are you?"

"Just along here, not very far," he said.

They stopped outside his room and came face to face.

"It's been a very pleasant evening. I've so much enjoyed your company, James."

"So it has been," said James, "and thanks for your company and also for finding that Italian restaurant; what a splendid idea."

He hesitated, wondering if he should be so bold as to kiss

her but thought better of it and merely shook her hand and said "Goodnight."

"Goodnight, James," she murmured mellifluously.

He watched her as she walked off towards her room and hoped that she would turn before she went in. She did turn at her door, pursed her lips in the shape of a kiss which she directed towards him and giving a little laugh, disappeared.

James's heart skipped a beat or so he thought, as he fumbled with the key to open the door. 'What a sweet gesture,' he thought. He succeeded in gaining entry to his room and straightaway sat on the bed staring vacantly into the distance. 'She's eroding my resistance,' he said to himself, 'I must not encourage this friendship but how do I behave to discourage her and at the same time not appear discourteous?'

He reached for his hip flask, unclipped the stopper and drank no more than a wee dram of Famous Grouse. He placed the hip flask on the bedside table and went into the bathroom to ablute. As he was drying his face, he looked at himself in the mirror. 'Is this really the same me who's behaving like an idiot?' he said to the image facing him. 'She's so warm and friendly.'

As he climbed into his bed, he pulled the sheet and eiderdown over his head just as he did when he was a little boy, ostensibly to be secure against his anxieties. At the age of thirty-five he knew he should not be reverting to childhood like this. Perhaps Helen is a figment of his imagination and in the morning the satyrs and goblins will have dematerialised into the woods whence they came.

After a while, James emerged from the eiderdown and taking another small shot from his hip flask, said his prayers, asking for forgiveness and giving thanks for his good fortune that Milly came into his life to become his wife, friend and confidante.

He spent some time thinking about her until gradually drifting into unconsciousness.

Chapter 11

'See the chariot at hand here of Love,
Wherein my lady rideth!'

(Ben Jonson)

On a cold wet evening in February 1926, the young medical student James Steadman stood in the queue at the tram stop outside the Royal London Hospital awaiting the arrival of the No. 94 tram to Ilford Broadway. He was well wrapped up against the bitter cold. The lapels of his trench coat covering his ears were secured by several turns of his Manchester University scarf, and the brim of his trilby hat was turned down all round to avoid losing the hat to the wind. His hands were thrust deep in his pockets as he peered into the rain and listened for the familiar clank of the tram. Two pennies for the fare were held in readiness between numbed finger and thumb. He was on his way home to his digs after a very full day on the wards.

He studied his fellow travellers standing patiently in the static queue of which he was part. Wherever he went he would observe people, wondering what their occupation was and where they lived; he was always concerned for his fellowman – it was innate to his nature.

In front of him was a Sikh, wearing the familiar turban, who had put down beside him a very large suitcase. James had come across Sikhs before when he lived in Derby; the one he remembered went from door to door selling brushes and cleaning materials. An elderly couple carrying shopping baskets were at the front of the queue and just behind them a priest in a black biretta talking to a dungareed workman wearing a heavy gas company overcoat. The latter was on his way to start his night shift.

At last the tram came into view, its solitary headlamp lighting up the wet cobbles between the tracks, and came to a shuddering halt beside the now animated queue shuffling and preparing to board.

"Plenty of room on top," said the cheerful conductor who thoughtfully helped the elderly couple on to the tram platform and offered to stow their shopping as they found seats inside.

James climbed the iron stairway to the top deck, pulling on the spiral handrails to hasten his ascent. He took a seat near the front and sat down, unwinding his scarf as he did so. He found that he was seated behind a young woman who was noticeable by her distinctive red and green Paisley patterned headscarf. The repeated teardrop pattern intrigued him so he leaned forward for closer inspection. The scarf was silk and the pattern woven, not printed, which suggested Liberty's quality.

"Fares please," called out the conductor which made James straighten-up sharply.

"Ilford Broadway, please," said James offering his tuppence. The conductor duly removed a 2d ticket from his hand held rack, placed it in the ticket punch strapped to his chest and, having made the appropriate alignment, effected a neatly punched hole in the space adjacent the words 'Ilford Broadway', the machine simultaneously producing a satisfying 'ding' indicating completion of the transaction.

The conductor moved forwards and called out:

"Any more fares please?"

The Paisley covered head moved from a forward-looking position for a brief moment to look at the conductor who acknowledged with a nod that the fare had already been paid. The head movement gave James just sufficient time to catch a glimpse of the woman's face.

She was young, probably not yet twenty, and good looking with a fresh complexion and dark eyes emphasised by long eyelashes. He observed that her make-up was subtly applied, the lipstick not too bright and a gentle blush on the cheeks.

'Hmm,' thought James, 'she looks rather pleasant, I wouldn't mind getting to know her'. He watched her as she got up to leave and then hastily looked away to avoid catching her eye.

The following day James left the hospital at the same time in the afternoon. On this occasion the queue had a different composition except that the gas company workman was there again. Unlike the previous evening, the weather was fine but cold, with a full moon competing with the street lights. There were no other people waiting for the tram, so the workman, who was a friendly chap always ready to start a conversation, turned to James and said:

"Hello young fellow; ain't so bad tonight. It rained somethin' awful last night."

"I know," said James, "I saw you talking to the priest. Is he a friend of yours?"

"Nah," came the reply, "I've seen 'im around. Him and me was talkin' abaht the trouble that's brewin' wiv the coalminers. They say they've got the TUC's backin'. We could all be on strike if the Government don't make a better offer. What abaht you, will you go on strike?"

"I don't think so. I work at the hospital here. I don't think my patients would be too pleased," said James.

"You a doctor then?" said the man.

"Yes I am," said James.

They boarded the tram which arrived with the usual cacophony of rattling brakes.

"Good evening gents," said the same genial conductor as the night before who stepped aside to allow the workman to stow his tool case in the space under the stairs.

On arriving at the top of the stairs, James paused half expecting to see the girl in the Paisley scarf. Not seeing her there at first glance, he was pleasantly surprised to see that she was there after all, right at the front of the tram. On this occasion she was wearing the 'Paisley' around her neck. There were not many seats free but the one next to her was, so taking the plunge, he edged his way to the front and sat slowly down so as not to press against her.

"Hello," she said turning to face James who, not being used to being accosted by a pretty female face, coloured a little.

"It's you again," she continued, "I've seen you several times recently. You're a doctor aren't you?"

James was taken aback at this frank approach. He was not used to talking to women on any intimate basis and had never had a girlfriend. In fact, he had been so involved with his studies and so determined in his quest to become a doctor that he had quite shunned the idea of any friendship with a woman on the rare occasions the thought entered his head. But maybe this one was different. She looked pleasant and had nice dark hair, now that he could see her head uncovered.

"Yes, I am," said James, "I've been at the London Hospital for just over a year. But how did you guess? Are you clairvoyant?"

"It wasn't very difficult," she laughed, "I saw you last evening sitting in the seat behind me and as I got up I happened to notice the stethoscope inside your breast pocket. He's a doctor, I said to myself!"

"That was very clever of you. What do you do?" said James.

"I work for Yardley, the people who make perfume and cosmetics. I'm a sales representative," she replied rather proudly.

"That sounds a good job. Is it?" asked James warming to the conversation and to her.

"Yes, I really like it. I started by working in the factory but after two years they liked the look of me and asked me to move into 'sales'. The pay is quite good and I'm allowed to have some of the products as perks." She looked at him and asked: "What's your name? Mine's Millicent but my family call me Milly."

"Milly, that's nice. Mine's James, though just like your family they call me by my pet name, Jimmy. I think it is because they still see me as their little boy even though I'm nearly twenty-four!"

"Oops! This is where I get off," said Milly all of a sudden.

"Shall I see you tomorrow," he asked keenly as she started towards the top of the stairs, "Will you be on the tram at the same time?"

"I expect so. Good night."

"Good night," he called as she descended the stairs.

He wiped the window with his sleeve, cupped his hands around his eyes and pressed his head against the window to see Milly alight onto the pavement. They waved to each other.

Chapter 12

'Let us love nobly, and live and add againe
Yeeres and yeeres unto yeeres.'

(John Donne)

The meeting on the tram was the start of a wonderful partnership. Their courtship was a very gentle affair, the relationship
growing steadily throughout the following year. He proposed to her
at Christmas and she was overjoyed to accept. James endured the
nervous approach to Milly's father, seeking his consent for the hand
of his nineteen-year-old daughter, whereupon the engagement was
announced. Milly's mother Alice, having suspected that an engagement was imminent, provided the ring appropriate for the occasion.
It had been Alice's mother's engagement ring which she had kept in
her jewel-box on the dressing table but had never worn. The Victorian ring had two large diamonds, offset one from the other, in a
cross-over arrangement. The diamonds sparkled, as did Milly when
the ring was produced.

With the family assembled, Milly asked James to put the
ring on her left hand and as he did so the family all beamed with
delight with the exception of Alice who wept for joy. It was a very
happy Christmas.

They discussed plans, as every young couple does and agreed
that a simple church wedding with just a few friends would be quite
sufficient; in any event they did not have any savings since his rent
had absorbed most of his modest income from the hospital despite
his father's generosity in supporting him throughout the past six

years while he was training. The wedding would take place the following May; May 12th 1927 to be precise.

Milly thought her sister Dorothy might like to be her bridesmaid. Dorothy, who was three years younger than Milly, squealed with delight on being asked and jumped up and down clapping her hands together. What about a best man? James had not been in touch with Roger King for over two years despite their promises, but thought him to be a good candidate. He couldn't think of anyone else.

Early in 1927 James came across an advertisement in the December issue of the British Medical Journal which read:

Dr. Hamilton Hardwick, General Practitioner of Woodbine Grove, Penge, London S.E. offers a position to a qualified physician with a view to a partnership in a well-established practice. Living accommodation is available. Applications should be made in writing to the above address accompanied by a curriculum vitae giving full details of experience.

This would be a complete change from life on the wards and general surgery. On consulting Milly, she agreed that he should answer the advertisement knowing that she would have to give up her sales job if he were to be successful.

A letter arrived inviting James to an interview at which it became clear that Dr. Hardwick was in desperate need of assistance. The G.P. was elderly and in poor health, not a doctor to instil confidence in a patient with his wheezing and coughing. The poor man wished to retire but still had a large following of loyal patients he did not wish to let down.

James saw the situation as a rescue operation and an opportunity to attend upon the good people of Penge. There was however, the problem of money. If he accepted a partnership it would take several months before he would receive income.

Having discussed the situation with Milly, they agreed that he should accept what was a wonderful opportunity as well as a challenge. He would move in to the two-roomed apartment on the top floor of Hardwick's premises. With the necessary three months' notice of leaving the hospital, he could start in the middle of April and have the flat in good order for Milly to join him after their wedding day in May.

All went according to plan apart that is from the minor matter of a wedding ring which James had omitted to discuss with Milly and she was too polite to raise the subject. With a few days to go before vows were to be exchanged, a visit to Bravington's took place and, as one might expect, the very gold ring which they both agreed would bind them together for eternity was the most expensive. No other ring could possibly interest them. The money had to be found but James had reached the limit of his overdraft and as friendly as his bank manager was, he dare not risk irritating the generous man.

The only object of any value James possessed was his stethoscope which had been bought for him by his parents. Thus, the 22 ct wedding ring was purchased with money raised from pawning the precious instrument, which by good fortune was redeemed within the three month period agreed. Not for the first time had his stethoscope played an important part in his and Milly's lives, quite apart from its frequent intended use.

The wedding took place at St. Anne's, Limehouse, with Dorothy and Roger performing their duties to perfection, Roger of course being watched anxiously by James as, on cue, he produced the gold ring from his waistcoat pocket and handed it to the vicar over the ever-menacing cast iron gratings.

James and Millicent started their new life together in Penge, cosily ensconced in their flat with the north tower of Crystal Palace rising above them. A young couple starting out on their great adventure knowing nothing of what the future might bring. They were confident in each other, secure in each other's love and ready to face any trials and tribulations together.

The newlyweds permitted themselves a two days' honeymoon which they decided would be spent in their new home. They visited Horniman's Museum, neither having been there before, and were especially delighted to stand with a small gathering which had formed at 4 pm in front of the Horniman's clock to watch the mechanical Apostles parading on the hour, noting that one of them, significantly, did not reverence the effigy of Christ. On the final evening of their honeymoon the happy couple treated themselves to tea and cakes in the Grand Hall of the Crystal Palace and felt very grand themselves.

After an exciting two days together, it was back to work on the Wednesday for James. He was starting to become acquainted with Dr. Hardwick's patients, one of whom was a very aggressive-looking lady sitting in the waiting room with her sickly daughter. The poor child was covered in spots. The elderly doctor came out of his surgery to meet the mother and child. He knocked on James's door and, finding him at his desk reading through the next patient's history, beckoned to the mother and her spotty juvenile and introduced them to James, smiling to himself as he handed over his most difficult patient.

"I'd like you to meet Mrs Bairstow and her daughter Mary".

Chapter 13

'I would have fled from one but singly fair
My dis-intangled Soul it self might save,
Breaking the curled trammels of her hair.
But how should I avoid to be her Slave,
Whose subtile Art invisibly can wreath
My fetters of the very Air I breath?'

(The Singer: Andrew Marvell)

It was the third day of the Harrogate conference. The doctors, after an excellent lunch, swarmed around the door of the coach like bees on a hive alighting board; the engine phut-phutting giving encouragement to hasten boarding. The driver, clearly proud of his well-polished Crossley Alpha, greeted his passengers, giving the occasional salute with a gauntleted hand.

James hung back waiting for Helen who arrived looking trimly dight in a long double-breasted coat and swagger-brimmed hat.

"Sorry to hold you up," she gasped, as James assisted her on to the coach, "Shall we go to the back? I can see a seat for two there."

They passed down the coach, nodding to their fellow travellers who greeted them as they made their way to their seat.

"Do sit by the window, won't you?" said James considerately, "It's a fine day so the Dales should look pretty spectacular. The tops of the hills could well have a dusting of snow."

The designer of the seat had economy in mind and was obviously not an anthropometrist. James took advantage of his observation and gently lowered himself into position. He enjoyed the physical contact of his arm on hers, albeit with several layers of material between them. Being James, he analysed the effect. How is it, he thought, that mere closeness can affect the senses to the point of intimacy?

"How did you find this morning's lecture?" asked James after the coach had wound its way through the city centre.

"Very useful, I thought. There are always new techniques being discovered. I am never happy to arrive on the scene of an accident, especially if there is mud mixed with the blood. You never know where to start. I certainly learnt something. He had a good delivery."

"He made some good suggestions on administering morphine," said James. "That's always difficult, making a swift assessment; where to go in and what sort of dose. All very interesting." James fell silent for a while wondering what to say next. "Ah, look, our first sight of the Dales! Isn't the countryside wonderful? Just look at that view."

"Yes it is. You really are determined to regard this week as a holiday, aren't you?" she said, gently sliding her gloved hand around his arm and drawing him closer.

"You have found me out, you clever lady," said James with a little smirk, "I must admit that was my thought when I first came across the advertisement in the BMJ. As much as I have enjoyed the challenge of taking over old Hardwick's practice and building it up, I began to feel stressed and so I prescribed myself a few days away. Now that I am away from the practice, I shall worry about how the locum is coping. Silly really."

"I'm sure he's doing very well," she said and, resisting slipping into her 'doctor' rôle, went on "What do you like to do when you find a spare moment or should I say 'if'?"

"I don't have any hobbies, if that is what you mean. Rotary and Freemasons keep me fairly well occupied," he said.

"I was thinking of something less demanding. Do you read?" she asked.

"Oh, I see what you mean. Well, I do like my books, come to think of it. I have a huge collection I have amassed since I set up in Penge. There is an excellent little bookshop in nearby Dulwich Village called the Old Laundry Bookshop. The proprietor is a funny old fellow with pince-nez who tempts me with leatherbound first editions. I like poetry."

"Do you have a favourite poet?" she said, warming to his enthusiasm for the subject.

"No, not really, there are so many but if pressed I would have to say the Reverend Herrick, though Yorkshire born Andrew Marvell runs him a close second," he said.

"So there *is* a romantic side to you, James," she said giving his arm a squeeze. James was fast losing interest in the view.

The route chosen by the driver included a stop at the Clarendon Hotel in Hebden where he informed his passengers that a rum punch was ready to be served by the landlord. This announcement raised a murmur of approval resulting in very little hesitation to disembark.

"I needed that, I was beginning to feel chilly," said Helen as they returned to their seats in readiness for the final part of the tour, "I don't know what they put in that punch but I feel warm all over." The coach lurched forward and once again she held on to him, feeling very secure in his company.

A detour took them along what was no more than a single track to a high point in the Dales for all to take in a final view of the green sheep-dotted valleys and hills with the occasional cottage signalling its presence by a wisp of white smoke. They didn't stop long since it was very cold and time pressed. 'Time's wingèd chariot,' thought James but said nothing.

The tour ended with everyone thanking the driver for organising such a splendid trip, the driver again deferentially saluting and acknowledging the compliments offered, as one by one his charges left his transport of delight.

Chapter 14

'Be happy while y'er leevin,
For y'er a lang time deid.'
(Scottish motto)

Following the tour and the visit to the Spa, the doctors assembled once more in the lounge for preprandials and exchanged news of their afternoon's experiences. The collective sound of excited chattering and laughter gradually increased until a dinner gong was heard which caused a temporary lull then returning to the previous volume, rather like a murmuration of perching starlings when startled by a distant report. The diners filed into the dining room in an orderly manner befitting of their status, each beckoning the other to proceed before them. They took their places. Smoked salmon. Excellent!

"Good evening, here we are again," said James, finding himself sitting once more at Table H opposite the smiling face which was becoming so familiar to him that he was convinced he had known her many years. This time she was trimly dight in a blue satin blouse with puffed sleeves and a cute bow tie of the same material.

"I very much enjoyed our tour this afternoon," said Helen. "We had so much to interest us that I didn't ask you about your family as I had intended. What does your wife do, you haven't spoken about her much?"

"Millicent? Oh, she is very much involved with the practice. She practically runs the place single handed. She took over from Hardwick's receptionist who left shortly after he retired which was not long after I took over. Her help has been invaluable to me. I couldn't imagine anyone else being so efficient and at the same time looking after the boys as well as me."

"What about your boys? How old are they?" She persisted with her interrogation as she wanted to know more about this fascinating and obviously hard-working and successful man.

"Joseph is seven. He's a bright little chappy. He's recently joined the Cubs and looks really good in his uniform and green cap. Next year he hopes to go camping. As for Walter, he's just five and will soon join his brother at the nearby Church of England school which is only a matter of yards away so I shall be able to take him for the first few days. After that he will go by himself or with Joseph. They are nice boys, high spirited; not what you might call naughty, just normal boys, if that isn't enough."

He hesitated and then said: "I always feel a little awkward being enthusiastic about my children when I am talking to people who don't have children. I have so many women coming to me because of their anxiety that they are unable to become mothers. What about you? I think you said fairly positively that you don't have any. I *am* sorry."

"Goodness me! That's very kind but there's no need to apologise. No, I hope you don't think of me as hard-hearted, but Gerald and I took the decision to forego that pleasure as we were both ambitious. I didn't see myself becoming a successful doctor without applying myself fully. I don't wish to labour the point, but we women are still swimming against the tide in this male-dominated sea, if that is not putting it too strongly. Does that make sense, James?

"It certainly does. I didn't mean to offend," he said looking a little sheepish.

"You didn't in the least offend; in fact I think you are quite charming and you *care* which is so important. That salmon was nice."

At the end of the dinner the invitation to take coffee and

drinks in the lounge was announced by the head waiter in an authoritative voice affording little chance for contradiction. However, despite the implied imperative, James, with his heart rate climbing, plucked up courage and moved alongside Helen and said very quietly and as casually as he could muster: "I've been thinking." He swallowed. "Would it be too preposterous to suggest that we might have our nightcap, er, upstairs?" He couldn't bring himself to say 'room'! "I have a secret stash of whisky I use, purely for medical research you understand."

"That's a very friendly suggestion. What fun! I hope you are going to behave yourself, James," she whispered impishly. "I shall see you upstairs."

"Number...," he started to say. "I know your room number," she interrupted, uttering a little giggle. "I'll see you there."

They plotted separate routes to Room No. 51, she, after a brief conversation with the two elderly doctors who had visited the Spa and wished to know about her day, went to the far end of the building where there were stairs which serviced the ends of the corridors on each floor. Before climbing the stairs she looked around furtively to see that the coast was clear, made a close inspection of a huge festive decoration and, without further hesitation, snapped off a small twig. Thus armed, she proceeded to Room No. 51.

While Helen was occupied in her clandestine activity, James had arrived at his room by way of the lift. The curtain had been drawn and his pyjamas were laid out on the bed. He hastily tucked the nightwear under the eiderdown, arranged two glasses on the desk along with the hip flask, straightened his tie as was his habit and awaited Helen's arrival. He stood by the door in confused anticipation.

'What have I suggested?', he thought. 'I shall have to behave myself as she hoped. I am in complete control, I think."

At last, a gentle tap-tap on the door. Taking a deep breath he opened the door gently to see Helen standing there with, very oddly, one hand behind her back.

"Come in", said James looking quizzical. She was smiling and looking charmingly predatory. Saying nothing, she walked past James and turned as she did so, keeping her back away from him. He shut the door and faced her.

"You're looking very mysterious, Helen, what are you up to, eh?" he asked.

"It is the Festive Season, isn't it James?" she said breaking her silence. He nodded agreement. "Well then, stand quite still".

At that, she brought the twig of mistletoe from behind her back and, standing on tip-toe, held it over James' head. He was cornered. There was nothing he could do but to behave.

The kiss was delivered with perfect finesse. It started with a little peck as she brushed her soft lips against his; then finding no resistance, proceeded to press her lips firmly onto his mouth. The mistletoe fell to the floor. His arms which had been hanging loosely by his side came slowly to life as though recovering after many years being in a comatose state. He embraced her with both hands pressing gently on her shoulderblades. After what seemed an age, their lips slowly peeled off each other and they stood together, he looking slightly dazed.

"There, that wasn't too bad, was it?" said Helen with feigned sympathy.

"It was utterly beautiful," he said slowly releasing her and taking her hands in his. "I don't know what to say. You are an exceedingly attractive woman, Helen. As nice as that kiss was, I do think that we shouldn't become, er, too friendly. It's quite absurd but in just three days I find myself falling in love with you if I haven't already. But we are both married and have responsibilities. I hope you understand. What about that whisky I promised you?"

"I suppose I have to agree. It is just that I haven't been treated so nicely for such a long time. Oh, don't misunderstand me; my husband doesn't beat me or anything like that. It's just that you know instinctively how to behave towards a woman. That's what is so nice about you."

"I'm not sure that is entirely true but that is very kind of you to say so," he said thoughtfully. "Now, I think we both need that Scotch. I am sorry to say, madam, that I don't have your favourite malt. Will Famous Grouse be acceptable?"

"Of course. There, you see what I mean, you even have concern about my taste in whisky," she said as she sat down at the desk. James picked up the hip flask and poured equal quantities into the glasses.

"That's about enough water, thanks. I like your hip flask. Silver isn't it? It looks as though it has travelled; I can see a few dents. How did you come by it?" she enquired.

"It was given to me by my aunt after my uncle was killed. It has his initials engraved on it. Look, can you see." He gave it to her to inspect. "He was a Steadman too, his Christian name John, hence the J.S. I was sixteen when my aunt received the woeful telegram. He was only twenty but I don't suppose it matters if he had been forty, it was still a terrible thing. So many young lives were lost on the first day of the Battle of the Somme. Will we ever forget the first of July 1916? So the hip flask is very precious, at least for its sentimental value. So here's a toast to Uncle Jack and to us, Helen." He raised his glass.

"To Uncle Jack and to us," she repeated, holding her glass towards James to clink with his.

They sat for a few minutes looking at each other longingly. Then, as though coming to a decision that a dignified retreat was called for, she placed her empty glass on the desk and got up to leave.

"Thank you for the nightcap, James. You're a lovely man but I haven't finished with you yet!"

She kissed his cheek and left.

Chapter 15

"I am most grateful to your Chairman for his kind words of introduction," said Professor Atkinson, senior surgeon of Sheffield General Hospital, in front of the assembly of general practitioners on the penultimate day of the Harrogate conference.

"I understand that the papers thus far presented during the week have been for the purpose of bringing you up to date with some diagnosis techniques. However, this morning I would like to review with you the emergency procedure for giving relief to a patient suffering from a blocked or severely restricted trachea. I am sure you are all aware of the tracheotomy procedure and maybe later we shall have time to hear from the floor your experiences in this field.

It is regrettable that in addition to the prevalence of diphtheria, we still have the poliomyelitis epidemic with us despite the continuing research into providing an effective vaccine. All too frequently doctors are being called out by worried parents to attend to a distressed child.

The procedure, technically called, as you know, a cricothyroidotomy, should be undertaken only on a person with a throat obstruction preventing breathing entirely. This could happen not only in the case of the aforementioned infections but also, for example, if the patient has failed to masticate sufficiently and has completely blocked the trachea. I have known a situation where the windpipe was wholly overlaid by a slice of ham, which of course is completely impermeable. Furthermore......" The professor went on talking for a good forty minutes and was concluding with the description of the use of a razor blade and drinking straw in the extreme event that a scalpel and tracheotomy tube were not to hand, at which point Helen whispered to James:

"Have you ever had to perform this procedure?" Someone in the row in front of them must have heard her and turned to see who it was, frowning as he did. James, putting a finger to his lips, replied so that she could lip-read:

"Yes. I shall explain later."

By the end of the lecture most of the members of the audience were looking around to inspect each other's thyroid cartilage, trying to estimate how far below to make an incision.

As the Professor was being escorted from the room, Helen turned to James and said:

"I'm glad I haven't had to carry out that procedure in an emergency. I have in the hospital during training, of course. Did you say you had?

"Yes. I was called out to a four-year-old girl with diphtheria. The poor child had turned blue by the time I arrived. I'm glad to say she recovered."

"That is always the problem," she said, "We can only do our best in whatever circumstance arises. The general public often expect us to perform miracles; we hold a position of responsibility, nevertheless, we have to earn the respect afforded us. I remember the moment I became a junior doctor; patients straightaway looked upon me as though I could raise the dead!"

"I agree, it is a responsibility and I have a continuing battle with myself not to let it go to my head. I do feel confident in what I do and I enjoy making people feel good even though I may not be able to cure them."

Luncheon was served. Various jokes were made by the doctors as they sliced into their *steak au poivre rare.* Helen preferring not to join in and asked;

"Will you be attending this afternoon's lecture, James?"

"Yes I would like to because I seem to be referring so many patients with symptoms of cancer, particularly women with breast cancer. The trouble I find, and I don't suppose I'm alone, is that so many women come to see me when it has become fairly advanced. If only we could find some way of early detection. I am always encouraging my patients to check themselves by watching out for any signs such as what feels like a tissue mass, or swelling under the arms or even a change of the breast profile."

"You sound quite an expert on the subject," said Helen with a slight hint of flippancy.

"I like to think so," said James, quite unaware of the mischievousness in her voice. He took all medical matters extremely seriously. He went on: "The silly thing is that people don't go to their doctor when some abnormality occurs for fear that there might be something wrong. In some ways it's understandable. What about you? Are you thinking of missing this afternoon's paper?"

"I think I shall give it a miss," said Helen, "As it's another nice day I would like to have a stroll in the grounds of the hotel before the sun sets. I sometimes find it useful to have a quiet time just for thinking. Why don't you come as well and do some thinking with me?"

"That's very tempting and of course I'd love to, but I feel that I ought to stay for the lecture. Thanks all the same. Shall I see you at dinner?"

"I sincerely hope so."

Chapter 16

'Now therefore, while the youthful hue
Sits on thy skin like morning dew,
And while thy willing soul transpires
At every pore with instant fires,
Now let us sport us while we may'

(Andrew Marvell)

The evening's dinner was taken with the accompaniment of a piano trio playing music from the films. The non-vocal version of the song made popular by Jeanette MacDonald and Nelson Eddy in the film Rose Marie, set the mood for the evening. It was not wholly familiar to James, so Helen, as delightfully teasing as ever, quietly sang the words as the instrumentalists performed.

" 'I am calling you, oo, oo, oo; oo, oo, oo, I will answer too, oo, oo, oo; oo, oo, oo.' It's called the Indian Love Call. Do you know how it goes on?"

"No, but I can guess by your look it's something saucy," he replied.

" 'That means I offer my love to you, If you refuse it I will be blue'," she crooned pianissimo.

"You really are the naughtiest doctor I have ever come across," said James releasing the knot of his tie from his Adam's Apple with his index finger and looking around to see if anyone could possibly have heard. This was unlikely as they were again taking coffee at their favourite table for two.

"James," said Helen, "It's our last evening together, which is a little sad. Are you going to be a dear and let me share some of your

Famous Grouse tonight?" she pleaded charmingly, almost daring him to refuse. He made no attempt to say no.

"I have to admit that would be rather nice but you must promise me," he said wagging his finger at her, "that you will be good. No mistletoe this time!"

"I promise," she said, not very convincingly. "I'll see you in a little while. I must go and powder my nose."

She left James sitting by himself quite nonplussed. He toyed with the idea of feigning a headache but thought that would not be convincing and in any event that was a woman's privilege; then chided himself for his chauvinism. 'She is a determined lady. She must be so, breeching the male bastions to become a doctor. I am quite disarmed. Having been so concerned that life had become tedious and uneventful, I now find that I am faced with a momentous personal decision. I must stay calm. It's not as though I'm going to be shot at dawn.'

With these muddled thoughts he started to rise from his seat but found himself confronted by the two friendly GPs.

"Good evening, James," they chorused, "we thought your contribution this afternoon very useful.

"Thanks awfully," said James feeling cornered. He didn't want to stand talking to these charming gentlemen who had been enjoying the evening sharing more of their war stories together and, from their colour, had been enjoying a brandy or two. They had little on their minds except tales of the war. James, on the other hand, was convinced that they could read his mind. They could see James's jumbled thoughts as though they were projected onto a cinema screen and knew that he was about to entertain a lady in his room. He therefore felt extremely self-conscious. Little beads of perspiration appeared on his upper lip which he dabbed off with his pocket handkerchief, making the ambient temperature of the room an excuse. He attempted to make sensible conversation at the same time thinking about Helen. He eventually broke off the engagement on the pretext of needing to go to the cloakroom, being unable to dredge up any other excuse from the inner recesses of his brain.

Back in his room he set about tidying up the place to his liking, several things not having been put in their rightful place by the efficient chambermaid. He arranged the glasses and his trusty hip flask on the desk as before. He waited a good twenty minutes but no knock on the door transpired. 'Perhaps she came when I was talking to the doctors and went away finding no response,' he thought.

As he sat wondering whether or not to find her room, the door handle rotated and in she came very tentatively.

"Hello," she said, "did you think I wasn't coming? I did say that I hadn't finished with you yet!"

She was enveloped in a dressing gown, more functional than stylish, and was wearing carpet slippers; thus apparelled she would walk unnoticed along the corridor each morning and evening to the bathroom with her wash-bag and towel. But on this occasion she did not get quite as far as her room on the return journey.

"Isn't this being thoroughly wicked, Helen?"

"Possibly," she said, "but you must understand, James, that I have never been, what you call 'wicked' in this way before and I am not in the habit of picking up men. I have been starved of love for too long, you see, and I half suspect it is the same for you. I never expected to feel this way but you are very attractive to me and you have said you like me. Call it magnetism if you like. I do feel a little naughty but here I am. Anyway, please may I have some of your medicinal whisky."

"You certainly may, my dear," he said, as he absorbed the content of her little speech. "Shall we sit on the bed, it's more comfortable there?" He had resigned himself to whatever the future might bring. "There, that's better."

They clinked glasses and quaffed. 'This is very agreeable,' he thought, 'though she seems quite serious. Perhaps she has gone off the idea of making love. Perhaps it wasn't her intention at all!'

They had a refill. The whisky gradually drained away any inhibitions either of them had. For James, there was the added intoxicating effect of her perfume; Chanel No. 5, the same perfume which had assailed him on that close encounter in the lift.

"I'd like to snuggle down with you, James. Why don't you undress and get into bed? I shan't be a moment. May I use your bathroom?"

"Of course," he said and did exactly as he was bid.

She got up from the bed, turned off the main room light, leaving just the bedside lamp on, and went into the bathroom, switching the light on in there. From beneath the sheet and eiderdown, he watched the bathroom door for signs of movement with anxious anticipation. The door opened, much as a proscenium arch curtain opens to an expectant audience, to reveal in all respects, Aphrodite herself. Helen had discarded the nondescript dressing gown which had been mere camouflage for what was underneath. The carpet slippers were nowhere to be seen. She was attired solely in a translucent pure silk white negligée. With the bathroom light behind her, James was thrilled see the silhouette of her shapely body.

Holding the reveres of her negligée together, she advanced into the bedroom and stood a short distance from the bed in front of James who was wide-eyed with wonder. As if by magic, the silken covering cascaded from her shoulders just as one sees the unveiling of a monument or statue. This statue was alive. 'How sweetly flows the liquefaction of her clothes,' he quoted under his breath, as his brain recorded not unpleasant signals racing from various parts of his body. She was the perfect woman. He had seen many women in the state of undress but none like the one he was enjoying admiring at that moment.

"Do you like what you see, James?" she asked.

"Please come a little nearer so that I may have a closer look," he instructed. How many times had he said that sentence in his professional life! She stood there for no more than a few seconds, sufficient time for him to see that everything was where it should be, no mental reference to the anatomical wall chart hanging on his surgery wall being necessary.

"You had better examine the posterior side, doctor," she said as she turned her back to him and slipped under the sheet which James thoughtfully held up, to take up a distinctly 'Venus at Toilette' pose whilst supporting her head with her left elbow embedded in the pillow. He was grateful that the Goya image did not include Cupid although evidently the 'Innovator of Love' was present in spirit. James watched as she made herself comfortable. He saw the hills and dales extending beneath the sheet like a beautiful landscape.

"My examination is complete and I have pleasure in informing you that you are a very beautiful woman, Helen," James pronounced, feeling his mouth go moist with slight salivation as though contemplating eating a peach. He swallowed as he prepared himself to move nearer to kiss her back. As he edged closer he could feel the warmth of her body on his cheeks. He inhaled the haze of her perfume and savoured.

Closing his eyes, he pressed his parted lips against the depression between her shoulderblades and kissed her slowly several times. He thought he heard a little whimper or was it a sigh of pleasure?

For her part, she could feel his warm masculine lips against her back, his eyelashes sweeping her sensitive skin; 'butterfly kisses' she recalled her mother saying on being tucked up in bed and kissed good night when she was a little girl.

He parted her hair with the fingers of both hands and kissed the nape of her neck. "That is so nice," she said, and lowered her head on to the pillow completely relaxed. After kissing her neck he worked his way down her spine giving little kisses on each vertebra until he reached thoracic vertebra T3 or was it T4? He was overcome by the sheer pleasure of what he was experiencing that his instinctive analytical thought processes were malfunctioning.

He reached over her body and took her right hand in his and drew it towards him so that he could kiss the back of her hand; her arm seemed weightless as she offered no resistance. He teasingly gave a puppy bite on the tips of her fingers, his bottom teeth engaging her red enamelled nails, the incisors depressing the finger pads.

"This is wonderful medicine; more please, James," she purred. He responded by sliding his left hand under her head and bringing his right hand around her waist to draw her into contact with his warm body. 'Isn't that what the Bible says?' he thought. 'His left hand should be under my head, and his right hand should embrace me,' he recalled interpreting Solomon's Song to his liking.

All of his female patients appreciated his gentle yet firm hands. "You have such sensitive hands, Dr Steadman," they would say as he instructed them to dress after examination. He was aware that he did have sensitive hands. They had been trained to be super-sensitive detectors. He could find abnormalities such as tumour or a pocket in a sigmoid colon better than most consultants. However, with Helen, his hands had changed their rôle. The very act of caressing her was something quite different; the hands had become receivers and transmitters of wholly sensual feelings.

Quite suddenly, Helen turned over and stared at James, fixing

74

him with her half-closed blue-green eyes which had become moist with happiness.

"That is so beautiful and exciting, James," she said quietly, "a truly wonderful hors d'oeuvres; I would dearly love the main course now."

> 'She looked at me as she did love
> And made sweet moan.'
>
> (Keats)

Chapter 17

"Sleep on, darling man. You have made me very happy." Helen whispered, kissing her lover on the temple before departing in the early hours of the morning. He stirred and extended a hand towards her which she held for a brief moment, giving it a little squeeze. It was not the time for a post mortem on their love-making. Recriminations and remorse could follow later if they must. He too felt happy and pleasantly tired. He waved as she slipped away into the darkness of the corridor.

James awoke in the cold light of day. The first stirrings of consciousness brought puzzlement. These were followed by a shock of realising that he had not been dreaming, which caused him to sit upright, staring at the bathroom door whence the apparition had appeared. 'Dear God, what have I done,' he said to himself, 'that is terrible, how could I have been so weak and fall for her charms? But it wasn't terrible, it was the most wonderful experience I have ever known before. How can I reconcile what must surely be a sin with the height of ecstacy so enjoyable. Two human beings waging love, not war. How bad can that be?' So started the self-recrimination. No matter how he argued with himself, he felt wretched and sick to the stomach. He sat on the edge of the bed for a while not knowing what he should do, except that is, to pray. Still naked, he slid off the bed onto his knees, placed his head face down on the eiderdown which had so recently been used as a temple of love, and wept.

Just as he used to do when he was a little boy, he prayed for forgiveness, for his sorrow for his disloyalty to Milly, for himself, pleading for strength to live with the burden of guilt that would hang upon him forever like ships' drag chains upon launching. He said the Lord's Prayer which caused him to choke on the words 'Lead us not into temptation'. Would his trespasses be forgiven? He maintained the genuflection for several minutes offering supplication for all the wrongdoings he could possibly think of until he realised that he was shivering with cold. He quickly fought his way into his dressing gown, now becoming angry with himself. He could not believe he could have been so foolish. He went into the bathroom and saw someone whom, at first sight, he didn't recognise. It looked like his image except that across his forehead was tattooed the word 'ADULTERER'. He shied away, not being able to look himself in the eyes. He drew back the curtains and stared out of the window as though looking for help. His eyes gradually focussed on the middle distance. What should come into his field of view but a church spire surmounted by a large cross, the cross which symbolised so much to him. The Cross of Christ! Jesus Christ about whom he had studied in depth and by whose parables he had been infused from the cradle. He groaned in anguish half expecting to hear the cock crow. What was he to do? He had the respect of his family, patients, church community, Rotary and Freemason friends- they had made him Master of his Lodge for heavens' sake- and there is Milly, his faithful and loyal Milly, mother of his dear young sons. The edifice had after all been built on sand and it fell; and great was the fall of it.

Having spent some time chiding himself, the doctor decided that he must face the consequences of his actions. He was made of sterner stuff than a self-pitying coward. The self-flagellation must stop. He had come up against difficulties in the past and who knows what troubles might lie ahead.

"Good morning, Helen," said James, a little self-consciously. She had been sitting on a chaise longue in the, by now, empty corridor, patiently waiting for him to come out of his room. Her mood was conciliatory and not at all like a female spider vibrating on her web ready to devour her prey. She had already done that, though in the nicest possible way.

"How are you this morning?" she asked, "I am sorry that I bullied you. I do hope you have no regrets. I certainly have none."

"At this precise moment, I really don't know what I think or how to answer," he said, "I do have some regrets which I shall have to live with and I don't wish to dwell on them right now. But how can I say, looking at you now as I am, that I regret anything. We have had a wonderful time together. You have given me joy, a greater insight into my own mind and a greater understanding of human nature. I have learned something in more ways than one."

"So have I. I am now determined not to be 'naughty', as you put it so sweetly," said Helen, now becoming a little sad as parting time was approaching. "I have had my little taste of freedom; I shall now return home and continue being the loving wife that I am. There are many ways of being loyal, you know."

"I suppose you are right. I had not thought of it that way. I too shall return and try to mend my foolish ways. I have been expecting too much of Milly even though she has a strong character." As he said those words, his mind turned to Milly and wondered if she would accept his admission of adultery. How 'strong' should he expect her to be.

"Maybe it is now time to say *adieu*, though I would rather it be *au revoir*," sighed Helen, touching his arm. That 'touch', he would miss that so much.

"I'm afraid it will have to be 'adieu'," he said regretfully. "It may seem very selfish and I am very flattered, but I don't think I could quite cope. If I saw you again I would want to see you more and more. Where would that end? Catastrophes all around! No, I am determined to carry on as before and accept the routine and mundane and be grateful for all the good things. I have been very fortunate and from now it is the quiet life for me."

"Of course you are right. I wouldn't have expected you to think otherwise. I am so pleased to have met you and shall forever be grateful to you for these few days of pure joy. Now I think I must leave before I burst into tears. I am supposed to be composed but even doctors should be allowed feelings. So it's *adieu*, James, and thank you. I shall never forget you."

They rose from the chaise longue and shook hands. It occurred to him that shaking hands was ridiculously formal after being so close, so he kissed her cheek, that oh so soft cheek of the face which brought out the sun when it smiled and which launched him into the stratosphere to take a glimpse of heaven. She turned away looking a little tearful and walked down the stairs.

"Goodbye, lovely lady," said James as he watched her go out of his life forever.

Chapter 18

'Love only occupies the brain,
That once could think of dinner.'

(PG Wodehouse)

Christmas 1936 was, to say the least, difficult for James and Millicent, though they did make a great effort for the boys who received the best presents they had ever had including a bumper Meccano set and steam engine. He bought Milly a bottle of the latest French *parfum,* definitely not Chanel. He had withheld his confession from her for several days after his return as he felt sick with worry as to how she would react. The purchase of expensive presents raised an eyebrow, but it was his loss of appetite over his missing the Devonian doctor, that finally convinced her he was holding something back.

He made his confession, trying to play it down by saying that it was all a moment of madness and it didn't really mean anything, which of course was a lie.

"How could you do this to me, Jimmy," she said, through her tears, "you promised me that you would never do anything again like that after that affair at the hospital." The brief affair was a mild flirtation he had had with a theatre nurse at Lewisham hospital during a series of days in surgery, but on that occasion sense by both parties prevailed.

He had apologised to her for his misdeeds, he told her how much he loved her, he said he had missed her while away, he bought her the biggest bunch of red roses they had in the florist's, and was most emphatic that he had definitely resolved never to be disloyal to her again.

The discussion between them did not become heated as they were both people of even temperament and had lived and worked smoothly together for the best part of ten years since their marriage. She said that she may forgive him in time but for the moment it was too soon after the shock of the event. There was not much she could do in reality; she had the boys to look after and the house and surgery to manage. Apart from that, despite his faults, particularly this recent event, she liked him. He had always been her close friend. She simply could not pick up the first stone to throw!

With Christmas over and the New Year bringing hope of a fresh beginning, the Steadmans bought a large house in Laurel Grove, Penge. The five-bedroomed house included an integral stable which they converted to a surgery with a separate entrance and waiting room. After the move to these new premises, James buried himself in his work and Milly, diligent as ever, arranged appointments for the increasing number of patients whom she greeted with a welcoming smile; although for Mrs Bairstow the smile was a trifle strained.

Early in May of the same year, after several months work without a break for both doctor and receptionist, Millicent announced to James that she wished to visit her sister Dorothy. The sister was married to a Scotsman called Fergus who liked to play the bagpipes. Their three-year-old twin girls Daisy and Poppy would flee from the room giggling in mock terror every time the drones started wailing; the repeated comical scene had become a family joke. The boys thought the little girls were very funny and enjoyed teaching them to play at roly-poly down a grassy slope in their garden.

Milly and the boys were away for a week, she quite forgetting that the day after they had left was the couple's wedding anniversary, the celebration of which was always important to James.

James sat at his desk in the evening of the anniversary. He had just left old Mrs Greehalgh, still dying in her eighties but still paying his fees. He sat thinking of Milly and thought how blessed he had been to find her. He recalled the tram; what good fortune to meet like that. And the Paisley scarf, which she kept in the bottom drawer of the dressing table. With these memories in mind, he pulled from a drawer a sheet of his headed paper, checked the ink in his Conway Stewart fountain pen and wrote:

12/5/37

Darling,

Just a little line to commemorate our being married ten years.

When I think of what you took on ten years ago, sweetheart, and how wonderfully you have managed, I am more than filled with gratitude, I do appreciate all you have done for me, for the boys, for the practice and for everyone with whom we have been associated.

Even if you can't ever love me again in the way you used to do, I still feel we have quite a lot in common, which may someday unite us in some sort of living progressive partnership.

I really love you with all my heart darling although I am still a bit afraid of giving myself up entirely.

My love and best wishes to Dorothy and Fergus and the twins.

Your Jimmy

Chapter 19

'To-day I shall be strong,
No more shall yield to wrong,
Shall squander life no more
Days lost, I know not how,
I shall retrieve them now;
Now I shall keep the vow
I never kept before.'

(A.E. Housman)

For the next two years at The Ferns, James and Millicent did work out between them a 'living progressive partnership'. She gradually settled matters in her mind and came to the conclusion that men are sometimes little boys. He was kind and attentive. They enjoyed together the company of their many friends whom they regularly met in the church community. He loved the boys and whenever he could, would take them as a family for treats. They loved seeing the stuffed birds and fossils in the Horniman's Museum. As for money, she never had to worry too much as the practice had grown to such an extent that she could afford nice clothes. She liked to shop in Chiesman's of Lewisham and Medhurst's of Bromley. All in all, things weren't so bad, she convinced herself, and the pain of his 'naughtiness' was slowly receding. James was much cheered by the reconciliation.

By the summer of 1939, the practice had grown so large James decided to bring in a new partner to share the load. His advertisement was answered by four applicants. After the interviews and much deliberation he selected the youngest of the batch, a Dr Richard Harrison. He was about thirty years of age, a bachelor with no immediate intention of marrying, very good looking; an altogether personable young man. He had trained at St. Bartholomew's in Smithfield and had qualified as a gynaecologist which fitted very well with the practice.

Just as the Steadmans had been offered accommodation, they thought that the new partner would like to take possession of the top floor back bedroom and adjacent bathroom. It was no more than an attic but for a single person quite adequate. He gladly accepted the offer.

Patients were at first a little chary about not having their first choice of doctor but within a few weeks the mood changed. "Have you seen the new Dr Harrison," the ladies would say when they met to chat in the High Street, "Oh, he's ever so nice."

Within a few weeks James found that the new partnership was working well, so much so that he felt much relieved and altogether less stressed than he had been for many months.

"Milly, dearest," he said, "I don't think we have been out to dinner by ourselves for such a long time, why don't we ask Harrison if he would look in on the boys this evening while we tootle off and have dinner. It's a fine evening and we could walk along to the Queen's Hotel. What do you say, dear? I think you deserve a little treat."

She beamed. "That would be so nice, Jimmy. I really would like that. Is it a special occasion?"

"No not entirely but I have been very pleased how Harrison has been so helpful. It's nice that the patients have taken to him." After a little hesitation he said: "There is the matter of our relationship which has been much better latterly, I feel. It may be still too soon to ask if you have just about forgiven me. I am ever hopeful."

"I have been toying with the idea of telling you myself but I thought I would like to hear you ask. That way I would feel confident about your promise and that you really do love me."

"I fully understand. So does that mean you have forgiven me?"

"Of course it does, you silly boy!"

"I am so pleased," he said and kissed her. "Thank you dear. You are such a kind soul".

Harrison agreed to the plan. He had some referrals to write up and would look in now and again to see that the boys were happily tucked up in bed.

They walked along Crystal Palace Parade, past the burnt out wreckage of what once was a beautiful edifice, where exhibitions and concerts were held. Henry Wood had once conducted several hundred young violinists in the great hall. Now, only the ghosts of the performers played there.

"Do you remember, we had tea there during our rather short honeymoon?" James said as they strolled along arm-in-arm.

"Could I possibly forget. It was such a happy day."

They arrived at The Queen's Hotel which was very grand although it had lost its first flush of youth, now that the place was not used so much since the 1936 fire. James briefly recalled a similar hotel with fluted pillars and capitols, but banished further thought by sheer will power. The dinner was a great success. They even had a bottle of Moët et Chandon to wash their cares away.

"I trust everything was to your liking, sir and madam?" enquired the manager," as they left.

"Very much so, thank you," said James, handing the man a larger than usual tip.

"Thank *you*, sir," said the manager as he stared at the palm of his hand.

All was well at The Ferns on their return. The good doctor had checked the boys as he promised and assured the parents that they had been no trouble.

"They did ask for a glass of water and insisted I read a Just So story; you know, the usual ruse children get up to for delaying lights out. Otherwise, I didn't hear a peep."

"Thank you, Dr Harrison," said Milly, "I hope they didn't hold up your work for too long. Good night."

"It was a pleasure, Good night."

That night James and Milly went to bed a very contented couple. James was pleased to find that Milly really had forgiven him.

Chapter 20

'Hope was his only drink and food,
And hope extinct, decay ensued.'

(Thomas Hardy)

James, on receiving confirmation that Milly was expecting their third child, was overjoyed; quite forgetting his decision that two children were sufficient in the family. The happy event would signify a new phase in their lives; if a girl, she would be christened Sarah.

Just as millions of people were starting to feel that the woes of the Great War, General strike and unemployment were receding into the past, a sad Neville Chamberlain announced that once again the country was in a state of war with Germany. The siren's wail heralded turmoil to come on that dreadful 3rd day of September 1939. Those who experienced the Great War, even as children, as James and Millicent were then, remembered the carnage. They had listened to the radio in stunned silence about the invasion of Poland. What sort of world would there be for their children and for their new baby?

With the awful news of war being declared, James became dispirited. His depression caused him to retreat into his study where he would read the Bible and his beloved poetry. Milly did her best to console him and carried on in her efficient way. It was fortunate that Dr Harrison was very much in favour with the patients who, after several months, were tending to ask for him. James did make an effort at Christmas to ensure that the boys did not suffer as a result of his gloominess. Milly kept calm as ever, hoping for her husband to come out of his black cloud. He could see the pile of knitwear growing steadily, so she was obviously busy with her needles. She did her best to stay cheerful and sat listening to the radio and looking forward to the quickening.

On New Year's Eve, while they sat in the lounge quietly listening to the wireless, they heard a terrifying scream. Joseph burst into the room and yelled excitedly:

"Daddy, come quickly, there's water pouring down the stairs. I think it's coming from the top floor. Quick, come and see."

James became animated as never before and followed his son sprinting up the stairs to the top floor. A torrent of water was pouring from under the bathroom door and cascading down the stairs like a waterfall. Milly joined them on the landing just as James had partly forced open the door. Fearing what they might see, Milly sent Joseph back downstairs, telling him to call for an ambulance.

Dr Harrison was lying on his back in the overflowing bath with the taps still running. James's first reaction was to check the stricken doctor's pulse to confirm what was already obvious to him. He, poor man, had been dead for more than two hours. James turned off the taps and stood back looking at the cold naked body submerged in bloodstained water, with one arm hanging limply over the edge of the bath. He had seen many corpses before but to see this lifeless body of a brilliant young man who had become his close working partner, stunned James into silent respect and a feeling of deep sorrow.

On the floor was a sodden letter which must have fallen from the dying man's hand. James slowly picked it up and, though the ink had run, he was still able to read the significant line 'I regret that I can no longer be your friend'. It was signed 'Hilary' but the writing was so smudged that it was not possible to determine the gender of the correspondent.

This tragedy was a great psychological set-back for James. He had learned to live with the Harrogate affair whilst still harbouring memories of Helen; he had come to terms with the routine and mundane; he had won back the love and respect of Milly and made her happy; he had solved the pressure of work problem by bringing in a new partner. Now, with the start of war and the death of his practice partner, he was once again under pressure of work and failing as a husband.

On the Fifth of April the new baby was born; the event was greeted with much excitement by the boys, who were allowed to see their baby brother being fed and watched, intrigued. James was happy that the baby was healthy and feeding well, though just a little disappointed that the child was not Sarah. They christened the new-comer Richard.

James continued to work hard in the practice for several weeks and then made an important decision; in fact, a plan for a complete change of lifestyle. He contacted a panel of doctors in the Penge area and arranged a meeting to work out a scheme to share between them the three thousand patients on his register. He informed the doctors that he had decided to volunteer for the Army. The doctors agreed to divide the list and the die was cast.

On July 1st 1940, Dr James Steadman was appointed to an emergency commission as Second Lieutenant, Royal Army Medical Corps.

Chapter 21

'But when the blast of war blows in our ears,
Then imitate the action of the tiger.'

(William Shakespeare)

For the whole of July, James was subjected to a military training regime in an attempt to turn him into a fighting soldier. At thirty-seven he was about twice the average age of the new recruits in his squad. The sergeant on the parade ground at Aldershot was nearly brought to tears at James's attempt to slope arms to the count of three, no matter how much he bellowed and he, that is the sergeant, was very pleased when James was posted to the military hospital in Stoke, Devonport.

It was no disappointment to James to find himself in the familiar surroundings of a hospital theatre. He was using his skills and felt that he was 'doing his bit' for the war effort. He soon became popular with the other surgeons and theatre staff. Having worked at Stoke for a mere six weeks he was posted back to Aldershot to become Medical Officer with the Royal Artillery, the latter move making it very much easier for him to travel to see Milly. He was amused to come across the friendly sergeant again, this time seeking his help to remedy a severe sore throat. It was a good thing for the sergeant that James was not a dentist!

On a weekend's leave with Milly and the three boys, the sirens began to wail and the bombs started to drop from the skies. The Blitz had started and the Battle of Britain was about to commence. Goering's air armada arrived in force early in September. The bombardment and air activity were so intense that James decided he must move the family out of the London area.

James contacted the estate agents in the Berkshire and Buckinghamshire area and rented a four-bedroomed cottage in Whiteleaf on the edge of the Chiltern hills, not far from Princes Risborough.

Ivy Cottage was one of several thatched cottages situated in a leafy lane leading to Burnt Oak Farm. Joseph and Walter thoroughly enjoyed their new surroundings. The garden of Ivy Cottage was full of climbable fruit trees, mostly apple and pear, one being eminently suitable for building a tree house in which they would play for hours. They picked wild strawberries, tiny things which had a strong, distinctive aroma, and brought some back to share with their mother.

The nearby woods afforded excellent opportunity for exciting adventures, such as hunting tigers or tracking spies; the brothers being away for hours having promised to be back home in time for tea. Bird-nesting was of special interest to them and their collection of eggs grew by the week. They loved watching the cows being guided into the milking stalls by the farmer's son and his dog, and stood on the pens to watch every movement the farmer made.

The local education authority arranged for the boys to attend the school in the town. They went by bus and met up with the local children who wanted to know from their evacuee friends what it was like in the bombing and if they had seen any German aircraft shot down. The boys gained considerable credit when they showed the children pieces of shrapnel and, golly, a tail-fin from an incendiary bomb.

Milly had the baby to look after and would take him down to the village in his Silver Cross pram which was large enough to take on board the day's shopping. Apart from keeping baby Richard fed and comfy, along with her regular walks to the village store, life was becoming a strain. She missed the Laurel Grove practice which had given her great satisfaction, especially meeting the many patients who had become good friends and were always grateful for the help and advice she gave them. She was suffering from boredom and missing the affection she used to enjoy what seemed an age ago. She rarely saw James who, at the end of September, was transferred to No. 7 General Hospital, Leeds making his visits more difficult. He did manage to obtain a pass for Christmas and arrived Christmas Eve with presents for Milly and the children but somehow the spirit of Christmas was lacking in his demeanour.

After the family had finished their evening meal and the children sent off to bed, Milly and James sat on the settle in front of a log fire and watched the changing images in the burning embers as though reading tea leaves. She sensed he had something important to say and hoped it would not be anything like the great confession of Christmas 1936.

"You look very serious, dear. Has there been any trouble?"

"Well it's not at all what I expected, but it seems that our battalion is to be shipped out to Egypt very soon," said James, pausing before finishing his sentence, "And they need me along too."

Milly's face fell.

"When you say 'soon', how soon do you mean?" she said anxiously."

"We have to be in Portsmouth by January 5th ready for embarkation soon after."

"But that's less than two weeks' time!" she exclaimed. "What am I to do, I don't really like it much here and I am getting so fed up. The children are wonderful but I am so lonely," she said and started to weep.

"There, there, dearest, please don't cry. I'm sure it won't be for long and I shall get back as soon as I possibly can. This is exactly what I had feared. So many couples are being separated because of this war. It's a miserable business. Now that I have volunteered I have no choice. In any event, I must do my duty to the young soldiers I have come to know. We are all mates together."

After some minutes when Milly had time to absorb the news and dab her eyes with her hanky, she looked at James and said:

"I shall miss you. I know we haven't seen much of each other of late but I thought we had worked things out between us. It may not be perfect but I was happy enough to go along with our 'progressive partnership' as you call it. But Jimmy, we still love each other don't we."

"Of course, dearest, you know I love you," he said reassuringly, and put his arms around her. She rested her head on his shoulder as they shared a few moments of silence together watching the flames slowly die away to nothing.

Chapter 22

'Again at Christmas did we weave,
The holly round the Christmas hearth.'

(Alfred Tennyson)

Christmas and New Year were celebrated by the family with an air of determination; Hitler was not going to destroy their 'bulldog spirit' entirely. James's parents arrived from Derby to see the New Year in. They all wished each other a 'Happy New Year', though the adults wondered what the year might bring.

On January 5th 1941 James travelled down to Portsmouth and joined the other members of the staff of No. 7 General Hospital Unit assembling and checking equipment in readiness for the field. A few days later the unit embarked on a troopship along with seven thousand service personnel and sailed out of Southampton Water en route for Egypt. The journey took two months as the course taken was by way of the Cape of Good Hope, the ship zig-zagging to evade the U-Boats which were sinking many thousands of tonnes of shipping with great loss of life. After brief stops at Cape Town and Durban for refuelling, the men disembarked at Suez on March 9th. The Hospital Unit then transferred from Cairo to Alexandria where they embarked for Crete and arrived at Suda Bay on April 19th.

Milly, in the meantime, made a great effort in coming to terms with the situation. She had received no news from James and she realised that it would be many months before she would see him again. She made up her mind to find something useful to do when the boys were at school. The baby had recently celebrated his first birthday, the boys hooting with laughter at the successful attempt by their little brother to blow out the single candle on his cake; the flame was extinguished more by dousing than being blown!

By good fortune, Milly, on one of her shopping trips to the village, called in at the civic hall where the WVS ladies were holding a bring-and-buy sale. The Women's Voluntary Service had set up an office in one of the rooms for coordinating the placement of evacuees arriving from the London area. She spoke to the ladies on the stall who soon welcomed her offer to join them in some capacity.

"We can do with all the help we can get," said Lynda Buxton, a cheerful, large-bosomed lady who was clearly in charge, as the other ladies would look to her for authority to accept an offer for an item less than the price marked.

"Would it be all right to bring the baby?" said Milly, "He's usually quite happy in his pram but if he makes a noise I shall give him a Farley's or take him for a walk."

"Oh, that's fine," said Lynda, "We have several babies here. We sometimes organise a crèche in the back and take turns in looking after them."

The idea of joining the WVS appealed to Milly and within a few weeks she had demonstrated her receptionist skills and had taken over the register of evacuees which the other ladies were very happy to relinquish. With her new friends, life for Milly had started to improve. She was very cheered when she wore her uniform for the first time and Joseph, after recovering from his surprise, said: "Mum, you look really nice."

Chapter 23

'And we are as on a darkling plain,
    Swept with confused alarms of struggle and flight,
    Where ignorant armies clash by night.'

(Matthew Arnold)

It was late in the evening of June 1st 1941. James had led his group of wounded men over difficult terrain from Canea to Agia Roumeli to be rewarded only by the sight of their rescue ship steaming slowly out of the harbour. The group sat on boulders on each side of the track, holding their heads in their hands with utter dejection. They rested for a while until James heaved himself up and slung his pack over his shoulder.

"Sorry chaps," he said, "we did our best and we all made a hell of a good effort but it just wasn't our day."

"No need to apologise, sir," one of the men ventured, "Blame the bloody Jerries."

Another soldier sitting on the track writing a terse message with a stick in the dirt giving his opinion of Hitler, said: "What do we do now, Skipper?"

"I'm sorry," said James apologising again as though the whole debacle was his responsibility, "My plan is to get you fellows out of here alive, which means that we shall have to give ourselves up."

"What surrender to the bastards?" said the gunner with the stick, still writing his justified obscenities on the track.

"We won't have any discussion," said James, rising to his position as senior officer of the group, "My orders were to get you away from Canea as best we could. Failing that, we were ordered to surrender. At the moment we are still alive and who knows what happened to those poor blighters we had to leave at the hospital."

"So here's the plan," James continued, "We shall go down to the coastal road and walk into the town. If you have any weapons you must throw them away."

"I've got a knife, Skip," said one.

"That's a weapon, so bung it away," ordered James. "As much as it pains me, I shall lead with a white flag. We shall walk single file with the two stretchers in line behind me. The rest of you will follow. Be as quiet as you can. We won't take our boots off, we might lose them. Don't forget, absolute silence. No talking or whistling and certainly no smoking. I shall do my best with my German when we contact the Bosch. Good luck lads."

They set off down the moonlit track and soon reached the coast road leading towards the town. James raised his arm to signal to the men to halt. He ordered them to relieve themselves, which didn't need further bidding, explaining that once they made contact with the Germans there might not be another chance for some time.

Ensuring that everyone was ready to restart, James walked slowly to the outskirts of the town until he saw what he thought was a sentry post and a barrier across the road. He turned and whispered to the stretcher bearers telling them he was going ahead alone but they should keep a distance of about forty yards behind him. The message was passed from man to man down to the end of the column.

As James approached, he made out the silhouette of a German soldier against the night sky. By this time James was within twenty yards of the sentry who was looking around anxiously. James stood still. The soldier was very young and had been left in charge of the barrier erected outside a small building requisitioned by the Germans. The entrance to the building had been barricaded with sandbags. Voices could be heard coming from inside the building where other soldiers were playing cards and smoking. One of them stepped outside to speak to the young sentry.

"Alles gut?" he asked.

"Jahwohl, mein Korporal," said the boy.

"Danke," said the corporal and went back inside.

Picking his moment, James cleared his throat and called out in loud clear German:

"Hallo! Guten Abend. Ist jemand da?" knowing perfectly well there was someone there; he had been watching for several minutes!

The young soldier twitched, bringing his rifle swiftly to waist level and peered into the darkness. He froze in terror. He listened in disbelief. Again he heard James call out:

"Ich bin Arzt. Alle meine Soldaten sind verlezt".

His accent was good so the sentry understood what the voice in the dark had said, that there were wounded men there.

The sentry shaking himself out of his stupor, yelled:

"Achtung! Schnell!" which caused his comrades to leap up from the card table and rush out with their rifles to see the cause of the trouble. All the soldiers released the safety catches on their rifles and looked in the direction indicated by their terrified comrade.

Seeing the assembled group by now crouched behind sandbags, James called out once again:

"Ich bin Arzt. Alle meine Soldaten sind verletz. Wir haben keine Waffen. Wir kapitulieren."

Five German soldiers listened in confused amazement at hearing their own language being spoken so well and, distance between them considering, with such a good accent. They rested their elbows on the sandbags with their rifles aimed at James, who stood with his hands held high, still holding the makeshift white flag.

"Kommen Sie hier," shouted the corporal, taking control of the situation.

"Ich komme," called out James in the steadiest tone he could summon.

In an act of faith, James took a few steps forward so that he could be clearly seen by the Germans, hoping that they could see his Red Cross flash. The stretcher bearers shuffled close behind and the rest of the men broke rank and raised their hands.

James repeated his well-honed sentences and added: "Für uns, der Krieg vorbei ist."

So far as the doctor and his exhausted band of wounded were concerned, their fighting war was well and truly over.

Chapter 24

'Yet the first bringer of unwelcome news
Hath but a losing office, and his tongue
Sounds ever after as a sullen bell,
Remember'd parting of a beloved friend.'

(William Shakespeare)

Having had no news from James for the best part of three months, Millicent was delighted to receive a postcard James had written when he was in Cape Town. It was a picture of the Table Mountain. The message made a brief reference to the jolly time they all had dressing up and entertaining themselves as the ship crossed the equator for the first time. She propped it on the mantelpiece against the clock and paused to think of him until she glanced at the clock to remind her that she was due at the civic hall in an hour's time.

"I've had a card from Jimmy," she said to Lynda Buxton.

"Have you dear? That's nice. It must be a great comfort to you to know he's all right."

"Yes it is, but I have no idea where he is now. It has been such a long time that I hardly dare think about him. I know it must sound terrible, Lynda, but I have done quite the opposite so that I don't fret and have tried to blot him out of my mind. In some ways the postcard didn't help."

The weeks went by and Milly, now happily occupied with the WVS and her new friends, contented herself with the routine of looking after the boys and meeting the regular intake of evacuees. In early June, once again sitting at her desk checking the availability of families willing to, or having to, accept London children, the village postman arrived with more official letters marked OHMS. He usually had a little chat with Lynda before carrying on with his deliveries.

"Oi bet some poor soul's in trouble," he said, in a stage whisper, "Oi was deliverin' the post up in the lane leading to Burnt Oak Farm, when I seed the telegram fellow on 'is modorbike. 'Ee called at Ivy Cardage but no one were in."

"Shhh," said Lynda quickly interrupting him, "that's where one of our ladies lives. She's in the back room here. Leave it to me. Stanley, I wonder if you could have a word with them at the Post Office to see if the lad could deliver it this afternoon."

"Oi've finished me round. Oi'l ride up with it straight away, Mrs Buxton."

Lynda, always concerned for her fellow creatures, prepared herself for the task of reporting what the postman had seen. Milly was in the office settling the baby in the pram getting ready to leave.

"I shall be off now, Lynda."

"I don't want to bother you, dear, but it seems that an urgent letter arrived at your house while you were here. The postman said he would deliver it very soon."

"I think I can guess what it is," said Milly, the blood draining from her cheeks, "I've been half expecting this. Was it a telegram?"

"Yes, I think so," said Lynda, who was feeling distressed that she was not really helping the situation. "Would you like me to walk back home with you, dear?"

"Yes please Lynda, if you wouldn't mind. That's very kind."

By the time the two women arrived at Ivy Cottage, there was the postman looking very red and a little anxious; his bicycle propped against the wicket fence. He handed the telegram to Milly, and giving a little embarrassed half bow, mounted his cycle and departed, feeling that he had played his part in this local drama.

The telegram was indeed addressed to Milly. She held it in her hand as Lynda sat with her on the settee trying to console her.

"You mustn't give up hope, dear," said Lynda, "It just says 'MISSING IN ACTION JUNE 1ST'. Shall I make you a nice cup of tea? We can have a little chat." Poor Lynda could think of nothing more helpful to say.

"Thank you, you're very kind," she sobbed, "Just as I had said to you I was trying not to think of him. I feel so awful."

Unknown to Milly, James was missing but not dead, thanks in greater part to his knowledge of the German language. He would be ever grateful to Roger and his family for all the practice he had with them while holidaying in Siegen.

James and his tired men, most with unattended wounds, were soon bundled into trucks and driven to a detention camp in Lower Galatas where they were herded together with many other Allied soldiers who, though captive, were also lucky enough to be alive, some only just.

On July 1st 1941 while still a POW in Crete, James William Steadman was promoted to War Substantive Captain. By this time the overworked motorcycling harbinger of gloom had followed his abortive visit to Ivy Cottage with the less harrowing missive from the War Office.

Chapter 25

'Across the wires the electric message came.'

(Alfred Austin)

Milly returned to the centre later in the afternoon so that she could phone her parents to tell them that James was missing and to reassure them that there was no need for them to travel to see her. She asked them to pass on the news to James's parents. Having thanked Lynda for her kindness, she went to the bus stop to wait for the boys and stood wondering what she would say to them. She decided to say nothing. They were happily involved with their little world and, as they leapt off the bus with hoots of pleasure to see their mother, she felt justified in her decision.

The boys ran past her as she opened the door, quite ignoring the letter which had arrived in the afternoon's delivery; they could not get into the garden fast enough to see the rabbits and poke carrots through the mesh of their hutch. Milly recognised James's handwriting and eagerly snatched up the envelope from the doormat. She took it into the kitchen, drew back a chair and sat staring at the letter for a few seconds. She turned the envelope over and read MIDDLE EAST FORCES written in bold capital letters. She opened the letter carefully and unfolded it once and then again. It was dated 12th May 1941 and began 'Darlingest'. Poor Milly, she burst into tears.

Milly, realising that the boys would soon be wanting their tea and might come in to see her crying, wiped her eyes and sat at the table for a moment to collect her thoughts. As much as she loved James, she was angry with him for having done 'a lot of very silly things'. The latest 'thing' had been unbelievably 'silly'. She had done her very best to accommodate all his interests. Being a doctor was important and demanding; she accepted that he should have other activities to ameliorate the constant pressure of work, they would make him a more interesting person. She accepted too that she had been fortunate in enjoying a privileged life, though his being so involved in church, Rotary, Freemasons made her feel, for much of the time, very lonely. Now once again he had been 'a little boy' and got himself into serious trouble, albeit inadvertently.

She looked at the date of the letter, 12th May and calculated that within twenty days of writing the letter she held in her hand, he had been reported missing. As she was counting the days on her fingers, the boys ran into the kitchen, shouting. They had seen the motorcycling harbinger of gloom roaring up the track towards the cottage. As the engine stopped so nearly did Milly's heart. Another telegram from the War Office.

It read: WE REGRET TO INFORM YOU THAT LIEUTEN-ANT JAMES WILLIAM STEADMAN WAS TAKEN PRISONER ON 1ST JUNE 1941.

Relieved with the news that James was alive, she said very quietly:

"Jimmy, you silly little boy."

Chapter 26

'The worst solitude is to be destitute of sincere friendship.'
(Francis Bacon)

Content in the knowledge that James was alive, Milly determined to concentrate on her work with the WVS. Lynda had become a reliable friend who would listen to Milly sympathetically. Lynda's husband had died, she preferred 'lost', ten years before and knew what it was like to be lonely in the sense of being without the 'other half'. She had loved her late husband who had a puppy-dog-like devotion for her. For him the golf club and occasional sailing trips had been mere incidental distractions from his lovely Lynda. By an extraordinary combination of nature and nurture, Lynda was a person of true British grit and unfettered compassion.

Milly's character had been toughened by the circumstances of being married to a brilliant single-minded and talented man whom everyone admired and looked up to. She had become inured to his determination in each and every passion he entered into though this did not mean that she necessarily approved of all he did. She thought Freemasonry to be very odd but went along with it because he enjoyed the respect of his male companions; the Ladies' Nights were very enjoyable. Despite the difficulties, she loved him and his passions, with some reservations, and had contented herself with bringing up the boys, who gave her great joy, and the WVS. She did find great comfort in Lynda's friendship and that of the ladies in her team, many of whom were enduring similar problems. On reflection, she thought, life could be worse.

One afternoon in early August, while waiting for the boys to return from the farm after milking time, Milly heard a man's voice, although too far away to hear what he was saying. She pulled the parlour curtains to one side to see Joseph talking to a fair-haired man in RAF uniform. He had been enquiring as to the whereabouts of Mrs Steadman. Walter had been attracted to the man's motorcar and was fascinated to see that it was one he had not found in his Boys' Book of Cars. As Walter made his tour of inspection around the MG Pb 4-seater tourer, Milly opened the front door and said:

"Good afternoon, may I help you?"

The man turned towards her: "I have just been asking your son if Mrs Steadman..."

"Good heavens! Roger! I hardly recognised you! What are you doing here. Come in," said Milly, quite astonished. "So nice to see you. Come in, come in."

A beaming Roger swept his cap in one movement from his head to under his arm, stepped over the 'welcome' mat and entered the parlour, offering his hand for Milly to take.

"How are you, Milly dear? I heard from the surgery that Jimmy is a POW and simply had to come and see you. I hope you don't mind."

"Mind? Goodness me no, I'm so pleased to see you. It's been such a long time. Did you come far?"

There was so much to talk about. She invited Roger into the kitchen while she prepared some cucumber and paste sandwiches for the boys and offered Roger tea and cake which he gladly accepted.

Milly told him how upsetting it had been for her to receive the telegrams and how kind Mrs Buxton had been. She told him about her work with WVS and how the evacuee children were finding rural life in Buckinghamshire. She told him how she placed a brother and sister with Mrs Whitfield, a kindly German lady who was married to an Englishman and thought how bizarre it was that the English children should be looked after by a German. Roger empathised, being half German himself.

Roger had been teaching at Felsted until volunteering for the RAF in 1940 as did James. Because of his knowledge of German he was seconded to Intelligence but, of course, it was all too hush-hush to tell Milly much about it. He had been commissioned as a Flight Lieutenant, the rank signifying his status rather than aviating. He was stationed at Medmenham, just eighteen miles away so reassured her that the journey had been a mere piece of cake.

"Just like this," he joked as he held a slice of Milly's sponge cake, "Delicious."

For Millicent, it was such a pleasure to see Roger again. She knew that James and he were good friends during school days and apart from seeing him briefly at the time of the wedding fourteen years before, she had heard little about him. He told her that he could not stay long but wondered if he could pay her a visit and take her and the family out for a ride in the MG. His work was obviously very special as he was not without a plentiful supply of petrol coupons. He was not available at the weekend but a time was agreed for Saturday week. The boys, when informed of the proposal, thought it a wizard idea.

Roger said his goodbyes and left in a cloud of dust, the boys waving as the classy MG disappeared down the lane. Milly went back indoors to find Richard grinning and covered in raspberry jam which looked at first sight as though the poor child had cut himself. The remains of the sponge cake, which appeared to have exploded, lay distributed in and around his playpen; so much for being ignored while attention had been paid to the handsome visitor as he departed.

Such excitement! Milly was so pleased to see Roger and smiled to herself as she contemplated his return. She started to clean up the mess thinking as she did so that, at last, some pleasant event had turned up after all the disturbing news of the previous three weeks.

Chapter 27

'I knew it, when we parted, well
I knew it but was loth to tell,
I knew before what now I find
That out of sight was out of mind.'

(Arthur Clough)

Roger returned as promised and, since the weather was fine, took all the family to the lido in Aylesbury. The boys loved the open-topped car and Richard was thrilled to see his colourful windmill, a present from 'Uncle' Roger, whizzing round as they sped along. All three boys had a wonderful time splashing about in the shallow end of the pool while Milly sat sunning herself in a deck chair feeling very happy that the boys were experiencing the attention of a father figure once again. Roger was kind and considerate and, following the success of the day, Milly asked him if he would like to come to Sunday lunch the following week. Roger gladly accepted, he had rather enjoyed playing 'dad' and was pleased that his presence seemed to cheer Milly.

A lonely charming lady, missing her man, and a handsome considerate friend, recovering from a broken engagement, makes for a heady emotional cocktail. The mutual attraction was like the inevitable coming together of two hefty permanent magnets with their unlike poles facing each other or the crashing together of the twin crags of Symplegades threatening to crush the good ship Steadman which had once been holed below the waterline and had slowly been patched up.

The visits became more and more frequent, so much so that by the end of September 1941, Roger was staying most weekends; arriving on Friday night and returning to Medmenham early on Monday morning. On the final weekend of the month Milly and

Roger settled down to listen to a variety programme on the Home Service with Vera Lynn. As 'There'll be blue birds over the white cliffs of Dover' was being sung by the 'Forces' Favourite', Milly gave a little gulp and said:

"I have almost given up hope of seeing Jimmy again. I have only had two letters and no real news since January."

"I'm sure he's doing well. He's a determined fellow. I'm sure he will be back one day," said Roger. He put his arm around her shoulders to comfort her, and him. He switched off the radio just as Vera was about to render the line 'And Jimmy will go to sleep in his own little room again' to save her further anguish. This wasn't the first time he had shown affection and it was obvious between them that they felt very comfortable in each other's company.

"It is very nice of you to let me sleep by myself in the spare room but I would like it very much if you would come and join me tonight," he said.

"That would be nice. I do so need a cuddle. I will first make sure the boys are asleep and Richard is comfortable," she whispered; a mother's duty to her children takes precedence over all other considerations.

Roger came and stayed with Milly whenever he could and became so familiar to the boys that they regarded him just like a father and saw nothing unusual about the arrangement; in fact they saw more of Roger during the month than they did their own father over the same period as James had little time for them when running a busy practice. He managed to have most weekends free but occasionally he would stay at the station with the other boffins if a surge of work occurred.

One afternoon Milly, conscious that the regular visits by Roger were causing some gossip in the village, invited Lynda to tea to explain her situation. Lynda had been such a good friend from the moment she joined the WVS and she did not want to upset her.

"I thought you had been seeing rather a lot of that nice looking officer and from what I can see, Milly, you must have seen him once too often," said Lynda giving a little nod towards Milly's waistline.

"Oh dear, does it show already? I wanted to tell you before but I wasn't quite sure. Do you think me terrible, Lynda?"

"What's done, is done. My, you have been a silly girl. When is the baby due?"

"At the end of July, I think. I won't embarrass you, Lynda," said Milly, "I shall hand in my uniform."

"You needn't do that for a while. So, who is this gentleman friend of yours?"

Milly told her all about Roger; that he was her husband's friend at school and he was James's best man at their wedding in 1927. She said how kind he was and how completely relaxed she was in his company.

"He makes me laugh and, best of all," she explained, "he loves the boys. He is altogether a kind man and he makes me very happy."

As to what he did during the week, Milly could give no clue other than he was on top secret work and was not able to give any information in this regard. She thought it best not to tell her that he was half German or that might have really rattled the villagers.

"What will you tell your husband? Forgive me for asking," ventured Lynda who was beginning to grasp the history of the dramatis personae.

"I shall wait until the baby arrives and then ask my mother to write to James. I am so mixed up I wouldn't be able to string two words together. It's a bit cowardly but my dear mother has agreed to write for me."

"What does your mother think about you and Roger," said Lynda, probing interestedly for all the details.

"My mother is absolutely furious with me and she can't understand how her daughter can be so beastly. She is very upset for James after all he has done for me and the boys. She thinks James is a saint. But Roger is such a dear. Do you know Lynda, he said to me that he saw himself as temporary guardian of me and my children and understands that when Jimmy comes back he would withdraw and go back to his bachelor existence. For me that's a dilemma because he is so nice and I love him dearly. I think it will break my heart when Roger leaves. He would not leave without a great deal of sadness but he sees himself as an honourable man despite falling in love with his best friend's wife."

Milly paused after getting that off her chest.

Lynda, as wise and understanding as ever said:

"Perhaps you should just wait and see how things turn out, dear." At that, she gave Milly a reassuring pat on her arm and departed.

So it was that Milly led a contented life with her new man whom she admired and gradually the village became accustomed to Milly and her growing family. Lynda had been very understanding and was always on hand to help. Milly sent a letter to James just before Christmas and another at Easter but said nothing of the advent of her fourth baby. Peter was born on the 21st July 1942.

In August, Milly's mother plucked up courage and wrote to James, as promised, the following letter:

26th October 1942

Dear James,

I have been thinking of you so much over the past two years and have been wondering how you have been coping. I expect you are very busy.

112

It is very difficult for me to write to you. I didn't want to upset you by reminding you too much of home. But I like to think that the letters you have received from members of the family have given some comfort rather than depressing you. I am sorry that one of Cecil's letters was returned. It didn't say why.

I went to see Milly at Ivy Cottage the other day. It was the first time this year. It was nice seeing the boys. They so love the country. Richard is enjoying his tricycle and speeds around the garden on it.

I had a long talk with Milly who is very unhappy and regrets that she has not felt able to write to you because she didn't want to upset you. I'm afraid she and I have not been on very good terms for some time. After many months I missed seeing the grandchildren and Milly so I thought to myself why cut off my nose to spite my face. That's when I decided to visit her.

Please believe me James when I tell you that Milly has been missing you terribly. She says she still loves you but she has been so lonely.

The truth is that Milly gave birth to a boy on 21st July. His name is Peter.

I am sorry to give you this news especially in your present circumstances but you would have had to know the situation in the end. Please forgive me but I felt it only right to tell you now rather than the shock of learning about it when you return.

Now I've told you the news, I might as well tell you a bit more. I didn't see him when I went to Whiteleaf, but Milly tells me that your friend Roger is stationed at RAF Medmenham and has been visiting Milly and the family regularly. He is very kind and looks after Milly and cares for her. He takes Joseph and Walter on walks and makes aeroplanes with them which they fly.

I know it's not nice for you but I beg you, out of the goodness of your heart, not to be too harsh on Milly who is very much looking forward to your safe return. I hope that is soon.

With all our love,
Yours truly,

Alice

Chapter 28

'O that 'twere possible
After long grief and pain
To find the arms of my true love
Round me once again!...'

(Alfred, Lord Tennyson)

Captain James Steadman, having been held prisoner in Lower Galatas for two months from the 1st June 1941, was transferred with the most seriously wounded men, to Canea airfield where Junkers 52s were to fly the prisoners to Athens. As they queued waiting their turn to board, James noticed several hundred men in British uniforms working around the perimeter of the airfield under the stern eye of German paratroopers. They learned later that captured New Zealanders had been forced at gunpoint to clear up the airfield following the German bombing.

From Athens, James was taken north by train in a cattle truck to a camp south of Berlin, the first of several prison camps where he was to experience the deprivations many thousands of POWs had to suffer until their release in May 1945.

In all, James spent many months in each of four Stalags, the final one being Stalag IVC, the infamous Colditz Castle, where he met prisoners of various nationalities, some eager to escape by various ruses which occupied their time, others like him determined to endure the discipline and survive.

James was in some ways fortunate in that he was dedicated to his work which helped to keep his mind off family matters. Being a doctor, he was permitted some privileges and was free within the camps to attend to the patients.

In Brüse, Sudetenland, he found himself one of a few doctors attending to about four thousand POWs who were having to work twelve hours daily from 6 am. Rarely were the prisoners allowed to report to the camp hospital. The Germans had ordered the doctors not to permit many POWs to report sick. Sickness was rationed!

One private soldier had chronic ulcerated legs and was permitted by the guards to attend the hospital. In the darkness, with only a hurricane lamp to work by, a situation not unknown to him, James treated the ulcers as best he could, without proper medication, by swabbing the man's legs with salt water and wrapping them in paper bandages. The legs survived as did the soldier who was forever grateful to the doctor for his unselfish dedication.

Due to the RAF bombing of local factories, a stray bomb fell close to the camp wounding some of the prisoners, which added to their and James's troubles. During the bombing he stayed at his post in the camp hospital patching up the wounded with whatever he could extract from the guards. His ability to speak their language with his persuasive arguments went some way to obtaining much needed medical supplies.

In addition to his duties as a medical officer, James made every effort to care for the spiritual needs of his fellow POWs by organising weekly services in the camp. The services were held on Wednesdays and were well attended by the captive audience.

Correspondence between James and members of the family was sparse and, understandably, the post took many months despite the valiant efforts of the Red Cross. In September 1943, when James was in Stalag IVA, he sent a postcard to Milly's brother and his wife:

Postkarte
Geprüft 27 Stalag IVA
Kriegsgefangenenlager

Datum: 20/9/43

Dear Margaret & George,

It was really good to receive your letter of June 23rd to hear that all is well, that you have two boys and that you are now back near King Alfred. I'm now at a hospital far away in the country amid the lakes and pine forests, but alas! No hills. We're a mixed crowd, French, Poles, Serbs, Russians as well as British. Give my love to your boys. I hope very soon we'll be together again, drinking our Colne Springs and Henekey's sherry and driving the bumping cars.

Lots of love,

Jimmy xx

The letters sent by James to the family members were necessarily kept short to avoid falling foul of the censors. Moreover, James did not wish to think too much about Milly. He had absorbed the news from his mother-in-law about the extra baby, somewhat phlegmatically and decided to defer any thoughts of what he or Milly might do until this wretched war was over. He had witnessed so many deaths and seen so much destruction he could not bring himself to contemplate how he would feel later. His main tasks at that moment were to attend to the wounded and self preservation.

In the first few months of 1945, the POWs were receiving news through the clandestine radio receiver that the Russians were advancing on all fronts. From this they deduced that the race for Berlin was on and the end of the war was in sight, which news caused a buzz of excitement amongst the long-suffering inmates. James continued his ceaseless efforts on behalf of the wounded, quite unaware that his personal life had been complicated by another baby born to Milly and Roger on 31st March. The child was a girl and they named her Eleanor, after Roger's grandmother.

The Russians arrived on the 18th April much to the joy and relief of all; the official end of hostilities in Europe coming on 8th May 1945 when repatriation started among much confusion. James, though naturally relieved that he would very soon be returning to England to sample his much missed Henekey's, was in no immediate hurry to join the cheerful masses of now ex-POWs waiting for transportation back home.

Why did he delay? There is no doubt that James regarded his calling as a doctor to be the first on his list of priorities. It was ever thus, as Milly had well understood. Duty came first although perhaps there was a nagging concern that he did not wish to face the awkwardness of that first meeting with Milly after four years apart. He looked forward to meeting his three boys but was concerned about how he would feel regarding Milly's other two children.

There were many wounded still in the camp and in the nearby hospital and still more wounded men arriving by the day. He was not going to desert them and so made up his mind to stay on. By the time arrangements had been made for his repatriation it was the end of August. The main repatriation check-point was located in Brussels where he stayed for a week before catching a train to London.

On arrival at Charing Cross, he deposited his cases in the Left Luggage office and walked outside into the Strand to take in once again the familiar sights of London. He looked up at the statue of Nelson in Trafalgar Square and felt modestly proud of what he had done, recalling the words 'England expects every man to do his duty.'

James checked his watch; he was due to meet Milly for tea at half past three in the Great Western Hotel, Paddington. He had plenty of time for a little fortification, so he crossed over the Strand to Henekey's Wine Bar and, noting with pleasure the wine barrel with the clock face sign suspended above the door, entered. There, behind the bar, was the same barman he had known on his regular visits to London before the War. James was gratified to see an expression of recognition on the man's face.

"Hello sir. Long time no see. What'll it be?"

Chapter 29

'If I should meet thee
After long years,
How should I greet thee?-
With silence and tears.'

(Lord Byron)

James resisted the temptation to order a second schooner of sherry; the first one, though excellent to the palate, was more symbolic of satisfying his long-awaited yearning to be home again. He retrieved his cases and hailed a taxi which took him to the main entrance of the Great Western Hotel, Paddington. He was back in the civilised world and looked forward to adjusting to life in England. A confident feeling flowed into him until he thought of the reason he was there whereupon confidence briefly ebbed away.

A waitress asked him where he would like to sit. Looking around the tearoom for a quiet corner, he chose a table with facing settles and sat down to read a newspaper. He attempted to read, every now and again glancing over the top of the paper towards the entrance.

After what must have seemed to James an hour, though in reality only ten minutes, Milly entered the tearoom and was immediately approached by the same waitress who indicated where James was sitting. He folded his newspaper and stood up ready to greet her as she came across the room towards him not knowing if she should be all smiles or be serious. To James, she had changed very little except that she now wore glasses. She walked straight up to him and stood facing him for a brief moment. James, saying nothing, held out his arms inviting her to respond which she duly did by slowly putting her arms around his waist and resting her head on his shoulder, he in turn, enfolding her tightly against his chest.

He found his voice:

"Milly", was all he could say. All that mattered to him at that precise moment, was to feel her once again in his arms.

"Oh James, I have missed you so much. I didn't think you would want to see me ever again."

"Of course, you silly girl. I have been waiting for this moment for over four years. Let's just sit for a while and let me look at you," he said.

"I must look terrible. My hair's a mess with the wind," she said. James thought to himself 'That's just like a woman. The first notion that comes into her head after all the stress of the past few years, is that she's worried about her hair!'

After a stuttering start to their conversation they sat, one on each side of the table, and talked about her mother and father who had kindly offered to look after the children while Milly came up to London. She thoughtfully resisted asking him about how he had coped, she would wait until he volunteered information, knowing what a dreadful experience he must have had.

He enjoyed sitting with Milly once again in the comfortable surroundings of the hotel. The conversation gradually progressed to discussing the children, Milly risking, as she thought, talking about the two new babies.

"How is Roger?" asked James; he was anxious to know where he stood rather than any great concern for Roger's welfare.

"Oh dear, so soon," said Milly, "I've done all my weeping over Roger. We decided to part when the War ended in May. I know it is almost impossible for you to understand. He has been so supportive and kind to us all. I had to make a decision and trust that you would still want me."

"Milly, of course I still want you and look forward to carrying on where we left off. For the moment I don't think we ought to go into the whys and wherefores of our actions. I have had plenty of time to think about things since your mother wrote to me about Peter. Poor Alice! That must have been so difficult for her. Isn't she the kindest person? Thank goodness most mothers are! And who am I to complain after letting you down what seems an age ago. Milly, I have seen so many terrible things happen and such suffering that I cannot bring myself to fight any more battles, especially between us. I simply must try to follow Our Lord's commandment to love one another. There, I sound as though I'm preaching! Well I am, but to myself. It must be hard for you and Roger. I hope I can live up to his standards, as for all accounts he has been good to you and the children. I nearly said 'boys'. How old is Eleanor now? Six months? Tell me about her."

"She's sweet. She has long fair hair and one bottom tooth," was all Milly could say, trying to digest James's ideas.

"How about Joseph, Walter and Richard? Do you think the older boys will recognise me? Richard won't, poor little chap, he was still a baby. I may not be too popular after all this time.

"Yes you will, I am sure," said Milly.

"Milly, dear, after these dreadful four years, I may not be quite the happy chap you once knew so I hope you will be patient with me. I have always regarded you to be strong. I think you have enough 'little boys' now and you don't want me being another. I often think about the expression I used in the letter; you know, the one I sent to you when you stayed with your sister. Apart from making a promise that things would be different, I suggested that we may someday unite in a sort of 'living progressive partnership'. It sounds a little pompous now but I think you understand what I mean."

He paused a moment and said:

"Mrs Steadman, please take me home to meet my family."

It was time for Milly to have a little weep.

Chapter 30

'How do I love thee? Let me count the ways,
I love thee to the depth and breadth and height
My soul can reach, when feeling out of sight
For the ends of Being and ideal Grace.'

(Elizabeth Barrett Browning)

In October 1945, the Steadmans, now with five children, returned to The Ferns in Penge and settled as best they could. James started up his practice once more with Milly attending to administration, at the same time running the family. No mean feat.

The couple worked hard at their 'progressive partnership', so much so that on November 21st 1946, Milly was safely delivered of her sixth child, the most beautiful baby girl one could imagine.

All the family gathered around Milly's bed as she showed them the baby. James was overjoyed and for the first time in his life became emotional, moving his glasses onto his brow and patting his watering eyes. He had his Sarah after all.

During the following Christmas holiday, James took Walter and Joseph to London to visit the British Museum of Natural History in Kensington. Both boys were doing well at their grammar school and were taking science subjects for their General School and Higher School Certificates. They were both keen on biology. James remembered seeing the stuffed animals and all sorts of curious things pickled in formaldehyde and guided them to the human body section. The boys having seen all they wanted to see, asked their father if they could go off by themselves and explore other areas of the museum. He agreed provided that they returned to the human body display within half an hour,

Content to see them taking an interest in the wide variety of exhibits, James's attention was drawn to a large glass receptacle containing a heart. He had dissected many hearts during his medical training and knew every blood vessel. He stood staring at the organ and wondered why so many poets had been inspired to write such beautiful verse. It seemed odd that we talk about the heart as opposed to the mind. The heart, after all, is merely a mechanism, albeit at very clever one, for pumping blood around the body. It can't think; yet it reacts to stimulation from the brain.

As he was thus musing, he looked away from the exhibit and turned to see, in the next room, a woman peering closely at a show case. James's heart gave a leap! 'Surely not,' he thought, 'I must be hallucinating! I will never forget that face, so much like Vivien Leigh's, the red lips and those slim ankles. It is Helen.' He moved a little nearer to make quite sure, keeping well out of view. There was no doubt about it.

Fortunately for him, the boys arrived back and asked if they could go home. This suited James as he was becoming concerned that he might find himself face to face with Helen. It had taken him years to come to terms with his affair with her and he did not wish to fan the embers with their tiny spark still glowing. He quickly planned an escape route to the exit and just as he was leaving the human body section, a handsome little fellow of about ten years old, ran past him and called out in the direction of Helen:

"Mummy, come and see the pickled monkey."

SUSAN RUFFLE (NÉE READMAN)
COMMENTS ON THE BOOK

The novel, Colne Spring & Henekey's by Graham Matthews, is based on the life of my parents John Edward Readman and Winifred Elizabeth Readman (née Mott). I was pleased to provide Graham with the details of my father's life, so far as can be obtained from the available documentation and oral account. For the purpose of his story, Graham has used much artistic licence in superimposing the life of his fictional character James Steadman upon the historical account of my father's life. On reading the letter dated 12/5/37 (see below) from my father to my mother, the author may have read too much from the phrase 'Even if you can't ever love me again the way you used to do,' but he was given free rein. There is no evidence at all that my father engaged in any extra marital activity, although all things are possible of course! As for my mother, she had two children to show as the result of what she confessed to me, in the last few moments of her life, as having 'done some bad things'. I trust that nobody will judge her critically. I certainly don't; she was a loving mother to every member of the family.

Dr John (Jack) Readman

Susan Ruffle gives the following account of her father, Dr. John Edward Readman

At the outbreak of the war in 1939 John (Jack) was practising as a GP in 15 Laurel Grove, Penge SE20, with an assistant Dr. Davidson. In 1940 Dr. Davidson died and it was very difficult to get another assistant. Jack decided to join the Royal Army Medical Corps and it was agreed by the local health executive that John's patients could be redistributed around the larger practices locally. My mother, Elizabeth (Betty) Readman and their three children were evacuated to Cookham Dean, Berkshire.

John was appointed to an Emergency Commission as 2nd Lieutenant in the RAMC on 1st July 1940. After some army training, he was posted on 25th July 1940 to Stoke Military Hospital, Devonport. There followed several postings which are set out in the letter dated 31 October 1994 (see below) sent to me from the Ministry of Defence in response to my enquiry regarding my father's movements during the War.

John was working in field hospitals in Canea. After the German airborne invasion the instructions were received to attempt to reach the south of the island, and connect with the Red Cross ship which would be there to pick up those wounded unable to continue combat. The story told by John was that they walked, stretcher bearers, walking wounded across the island through the White Mountains, receiving help from the locals whenever possible until they reached Agia Roumeli where they saw the Red Cross ship sailing out of the harbour with the Red Cross sign lit up. The orders from senior officers were to surrender to the Germans immediately, whereupon

John approached a German guard (he recognised him in the dark by the outline of his helmet against the night sky!) and spoke to him in German.

On 1st June 1941 he was reported missing and on the same day he was identified as being a Prisoner of War.

He remained on Crete, at Lower Galatas until the end of July. (His notes which he kept in his medical book give the dates as leaving Salonika on 5th August arriving Luckenwalde 21st August 1941).

It has been recorded that the local women, wherever the cattle truck travelled, would lob bread in the air over the heads of the Germans for the Allied soldiers who were starving.

From here onwards the records have been gleaned from John's notes in his diary and his medical book entitled 'Medical Diseases of War' by Sir Arthur Hurst, published by Edward Arnold in 1940 (in the possession of Russell Readman, John's oldest grandson).

John was in Luckenwald (Stalag IIIA) from the 11th August 1941 until 29th October 1941.

On 30th October 1941 he was transferred to Steglitz (Stalag IIID) near Bielsdorf, which John describes as Hotel de Louise 404 and there is no further information whilst he was there but that he noted in his book that from 10th April 1942 until 17th December 1942, 'The Cage' Neukölln 401. He also noted a date 24th December 1942 to 21st January 1943 followed by the numbers 404, (404 being the reference number for the camp) then from 21st January to 16th August he noted he was at camp 428 Zernsdorf bei Königs Wusterhausen.

On 16th August 1943 he was transferred to Hohenstein (Stalag IVA) which he notes as Königswartha (LAZ 744) but was there for only two months, leaving on 20th October 1943.

Hereon, the records are confusing; the Ministry of Defence gives his movement as being transferred from Hohenstein on 21st October 1943 to Colditz (Stalag IVC) where he remained for the rest of the war. His diary entries are very cryptic, necessarily so and therefore difficult of decipher.

There is a photograph of John (see below) with his fellow prisoners in Stalag IVC in the records verified on the back by John in his own handwriting.

From his diary we have references to various places and people. The next we know is a note stating that on 25th October, for 24hrs, John was in Lager Columbus Shacht IVC. Then on 26th October until 24th February 1944 he was in Lindau IV.

10th March to 27th April.................Oberleutensdorf
27th April to 4th May......................Wistritz
4th May to 14th May.......................Mühlberg
15th May to 3rd June......................Komatau
3rd June 1944 to 20th May 1945 Lager Zwei Zwanzig

There is a note for Christmas 1944 where he writes 'Still in Lager Zwei Zwanzig. Dec 25th '44 The Suicide Squad 'then he names S J Cawood, Dr de Saim, F A Waller and R Budd.

He notes 'Sam's wedding' on 15th May 1945 Nieder-georgethal.

John was released from Colditz amongst great confusion. It was known that he stayed behind in order to medically check the combatants before their own repatriation and I believe that would have been in Brussels as there are notes regarding Brussels in the diary; it was a main repatriation check-point. He returned to England sometime after 24th May 1945 arriving at Cookham Dean in the September. He was released from duty 10th January 1946, and on

21st February 1946 was awarded the MBE with the honorary rank of Captain.

The citation reads:

'The King has been generously pleased to give orders for the appointment to the Most Excellent Order of the British Empire in recognition of gallant and distinguished services whilst a prisoner of war..........to be an Additional member of the Military Division of the said Most excellent Order: Captain John Edward Readman (136190) RAMC'

He returned to Penge and his GP practice in 1945 accompanied by Betty and the children. I was born 21st November 1946.

Jack's letter to Betty written on their tenth anniversary 12/05/1937

TELEPHONE:
SYDENHAM 7711.

HOURS:
MORNINGS 10 - 11.30 A.M.
AFTERNOON 4 - 5.30 P.M.
(SATURDAYS ONLY)
EVENINGS 7 - 9 P.M.
(EXCEPT THURS. & SATS.)

FROM DR. J. E. READMAN.

"THE FERS."
15, LAUREL GROVE.
S.E.20.

12/5/37

Darling,

Just a little line to commemorate our being married ten years.

When I think of what you took on ten years ago, sweetheart, & how wonderfully you have managed, I am more than filled with gratitude. I do appreciate all you have done for me, for the boys, for the practice & for everyone with whom we have been associated.

Even if you can't ever love me again in the way you used to do, I still feel we have quite a lot in common, which may some day unite us in some sort of living progressive partnership. I really love you with all my heart darling although I am still a bit afraid of giving myself up entirely.

My love & best wishes to John & Billy & Elsie.

Your Jack.

Jack's letter to sister Winnie 8/05/1941

M.E. Force 2.

Dear Winnie,

I'm wishing you many happy
returns of the day, but as you won't
get this letter for about two months
I'm afraid ~~you~~ I'll be rather out of date
unless you get my wish by telepathy

I expect you heard from various members
among our relations that I had joined
the RAMC last July. Davidson had joined
in the previous October, and I could not
get an assistant for love nor money so
I went to (see) the clerk to my Panel
Committee & he agreed that my 3000
panel patients would be better looked
after if they were split up among the
twenty or so doctors over 45 years of age
still remaining in Penge & Beckenham.

So here I am, somewhere in the Middle
East.

133

How are you all getting on? You and Roland, Tony, Joy, & Baby (is he Philip?) I do hope the raiders have not troubled Bedford too much & that you have been spared from the more serious consequences.

I am constantly coming across men from Bedford & Bedfordshire. We have with us now a Lieut. Quartermaster who was born in Cardington. One of our padres was for a time at Bunyan Meeting Hall.

Betty & the three boys are all quite well & very happy in their country home near Marlow. John was 13 last week & Bobby is over a year old, & very fit.

I am quite safe & well so far, which is a lot to be thankful for. On the whole I am enjoying life tremendously, but I'll be very glad when it's all over & we are all back home again.

Last July I went to Aldershot where they tried to teach doctors to be fit. They were not very successful.

From there I went to Plymouth, to a
military hospital for six weeks. So for
once I had a real seaside holiday !!
Then I went as M.O. to a regiment in
Wiltshire. I hoped I was set until then
for duration, but alas on Oct. 29th I
received orders to report to Leeds for service
overseas. So here I am in the M.E.F.

We spent some time in the desert where the
sand, flies, heat & mosquitoes were almost
unbearable. We had a fortnight just outside
an Eastern City of great historical & architectural
interest. We were not too busy & had plenty
of time to explore; it was marvellous.

Now we are in a delightful spot, by
the sea, surrounded by olive groves and
vineyards, with snow topped mountains in
the distance. The sea is excellent for bathing
& the country grand for walking.

We were very busy last week, night &
day, but one morning a fairy ship arrived
through the darkness, all lit up & carrying the
Red Cross. She took away most of our serious

cases, so this week we have not had quite such a rush. I like the work tremendously, but hate the war which makes it necessary. We can only hope that it will lead to a really new world of Liberty Equality & Fraternity.

Give my love to Roland & the children, & to my various relations in Bedfordshire when you see them.

With lots of love.

Jack

Jack's letter to his wife's brother Claud 11/05/1941

11/5/41   M.E.F. somewhere

Dear Claud.

I was delighted to find your letter in the mail on Friday night, and very glad to read its cheerful contents, in spite of all you are going through, and to know that you are all well, that things are going more smoothly, and that the approach of fire is in your capable hands.

We are having a grand time here; plenty of hard work, but still time to enjoy the really marvellous country to bathe in the clearest sea you could imagine & to drink the native wine which is almost as good as a Berskins Colne Spring or a Henexey's sherry.

I shall be delighted to act as Godfather to your baby son or daughter. only hope I shall be back in time

Then we will celebrate in great style, the end of all this nonsense and the beginning of a new world really worth living in. I'm certain the mistakes of 1918-19 will not be repeated.

These babies which are being born will have to work hard, but they will have something worth working for.

Here unfortunately we are very much cut off from the rest of the civilised world. — No newspapers ~~and~~ for wireless we have to go three miles to an electric cable. There are no batteries.

We have no candles, but we've just enough paraffin to keep our hurricane lamps going. Milk once a day, at breakfast. No bread or potatoes, but ~~to~~ substitutes dog biscuits and rice. It's great fun.

My love & all best wishes to Nellie.
           Cheerio Claud & all the best.
                      Jack.

P.S. I've only one envelope so I'm putting this in with John's letter.

Jack's letter to Betty, written in Crete on their fourteenth anniversary 12/ 05/1941, twenty days before capture

> 1.6190 Lt. J E Readman
> 7 Gen. Hosp RAMC
> TELEPHONE 2037/-2 MEF.
>
> LEEDS AND COUNTY CONSERVATIVE CLUB
> LEEDS
> 12 May 1941
>
> Darlingest.
> How are you feeling on this, the
> anniversary of our wedding day.
> Although you wont get this probally
> for another two months, I must write
> to tell you how very much I
> am thinking of you, how very much I
> love you, and how very glad I am for
> what happened exactly fourteen years ago
> to-day.
> It's the first time we've been separated
> on this day — yet, although separated in
> space, I feel very near to you sometimes.
> What a little boy I was when we got
> married! You were much more grown up than
> I was. I loved you then, as much as it
> was possible for a little boy to love
> anyone. In the growing up process, I did
> a lot of very silly things & yet, really
> I loved you all the time, even if I

139

John Readman (second from left) and fellow POWs in Stalag IVC (Colditz)

MINISTRY OF DEFENCE CS(RM)2b

Bourne Avenue Hayes Middlesex UB3 1RF

Telephone 081-573 3831 ext **320**

Mrs S Ruffle 41 Wood Ride Petts Wood BR5 1QA	Your reference Our reference 94/77911/CS(RM)2b/3 Date 31 October 1994

Dear Mrs Ruffle

In reply to your letter, our records show the following particulars of the military service of **Captain John Edward READMAN - Royal Army Medical Corps.**

Appointed to a Emergency Commission as 2nd Lieutenant in the Royal Army Medical Corps and posted to 1st Depot	01.07.40
Posted to Military Hospital, Stoke, Devonport	25.07.40
Posted to Nº.5 Corps H.Q as Pool Medical Officer	09.09.40
Posted to 5 Surrey Regiment R.A.	29.09.40
Posted to Nº.7 General Hospital - Leeds	29.10.40
Proceeded with above Unit to Port of Embarkation for service in the Middle East	05.01.41
Disembarked at Port Suez	09.03.41
Proceeded from Cairo to Alexandria	05.04.41
Embarked at Egypt	13.04.41
Disembarked Crete	19.04.41
Reported Missing	01.06.41
Confirmed as Prisoner of War	01.06.41
Repatriated to U.K	24.05.45
Released	10.01.46
Relinquished Commission and granted the honorary rank of Captain	15.03.54

It can be confirmed that he was Prisoner of War in the following Camps:

Lower Galatos, Crete	01.06.41	to 10.08.41
① Stalag IIIA - Luckenwalde	11.08.41	to 29.10.41
Stalag IIID - Steglitz (near Bielsdorf)	30.10.41	to 15.08.43
Stalag IVA - Hohnstein-	16.08.43	to 20.10.43
Stalag IVC - Colditz	21.10.43	to 23.05.45

① Due South of Berlin

We do not know if any of the above camps are still standing as memorials. You may be able to discover this information from the Imperial War Museum, Lambeth Road, London.

I hope this information is of assistance to you.

Yours sincerely

K Welbourne.

K WELBOURNE (MRS)
for Departmental Record
Officer

ss

Letter from Edward Ayling to Elizabeth (Betty) Readman

Edward Ayling
Mill Hatch
Trotton
Petersfield
Hants GU13 5JX

December 18th '79

Madam,

Thank you for your telegram, I much regret to learn of the captain passing away and it is my hope that my Christmas card was not the cause of any hurt to your good self.

I will never forget his unstinting effort on our behalf in Brüse Sudetenland. He had about 4,000 of us to look after. We had to work twelve hours daily, and he was only allowed to excuse a small percentage offside. He tended my chronic ulcerated legs with such care; he had little else but salt water, paper bandages and often only a hurricane lamp. Sick parade was 4.30am daily so that most could be pushed off to work by 6am. We were constantly bombed at the latter time and the men were getting wounded. God knows how many hours he worked or when he rested. How he did it we shall never know.

Today, all those years later, I have 2 sound legs, but for his unceasing care, no doubt they would have been amputated. I'm coming 63, and absolutely fit, and I wanted to thank him.

I hope I don't hurt you Madam, all the best and a Happy Xmas to you.

Kind regards,

Edward Ayling (former Private, Royal Sussex Reg't)

Letter from Edward Ayling to William (Bill) Readman

Edward Ayling
Mill Hatch
Trotton
Petersfield
Hants

Dec 18th '79

Dear Sir

Thank you for your kind letter of the 10th inst. I am relieved that my card caused no distress. In reply to your query, I left the camp 9th May 45, the day after hostilities were supposed to have finished. Anyway, you will see all about that – I will send along the diary when I can recover it from a borrower. Many have borrowed it and it has become a bit dirty! One fellow sent it to the Imperial War Museum where it was copied in its entirety to my amusement [- I am <u>no</u> writer!]

Of course, I was sad to hear of the Capt's passing, but as he did not tell you much no doubt you will glean a little from my notes. We were all, in the camp, so grateful for his unselfish attention. The padre you mentioned, now Canon Dunlop, ret'd, lives at Havant, Winchester (?) Sussex. I have never seen him since, and once when I telephoned he seemed reluctant to talk. I must call on him one day, about 12 miles from here.

Thank you for writing. The diary will turn up in due course. My respects to your mother and the family.

Truly,

Edward Ayling

Edward Ayling - extracts

The following are extracts from Edward Ayling's memoirs in which he pays tribute to John Readman whom he refers to as M.O.

> Those excused [from factory work – Ed.] were normally rounded up for work on odd jobs around the camp, that is, unless they were kept in the sick bay, or ordered to "bed down" in their own huts by the M.O. As I said, a farce, but no fault of our tireless M.O.; how he preserved his sanity, I can't tell.

Also, following his description of a bombing raid, Edward Ayling writes:

> 'The British M.O. had not moved from his post all the time; a better man than I". Yet again: "For the next few days there was peace, so our nerves gained a bit of a rest. Once again, there was no water or light, and the poor M.O.'s lot was by no means a happy one.'

GRAPEVINE - published by St Peter & St Pauls C of E Church, Bromley, Kent

The Lent 1980 edition of Grapevine Included an extract from a letter dated 'Lent 1980' sent by Ron Palmer to a fellow former POW called Bob (nickname 'Dean'):

> 'It was good of you to remind me of the medical officer [Captain J. E. Readman – Ed.] in our camp who, when we were released, remained behind in the Russian zone to look after his patients when all we were concerned about was to get home quickly!'

1903   John (Jack) Edward Readman born 29th October to Jack & Elizabeth Readman (née Humphreys).

Edward Readman owned a chemist's shop in Friar Gate, Derby. Both Edward and Mary's parents were neighbouring tenant farmers on the Duke of Bedford's estate near Brogborough.

1907   Jack's wife Elizabeth (Betty) Mott was born 20th September in Poplar, East London. She was the oldest of five children. Her father fought in the Boer War and later became a commissionaire at the brewery Inde Coope, Northey St., Poplar.

1913   Jack wins a scholarship to Derby Grammar School.

1920   He begins his medical training at Manchester University and gains B.Sc. in medicine (MB).

1923   He enters medical school at the London Hospital, Whitechapel, E. London.

1925   Jack continues his training at the London Hospital (see letter of recommendation in the Appendix) and qualifies as MB, LRCP, MRCS.

1926   Jack meets Betty on a tram. She worked at the Yardley perfume factory from 1924.

1927   Betty & Jack marry at St. Anne's, Poplar on May 12th. (Jack pawned his stethoscope to buy her a wedding ring.) First practice in Kingshall Road, Penge.

1928   Purchases practice in Howard Road, Penge.

1929   <u>First child</u> John Alfred, born to Jack & Betty on April 27th.

1932 Second child William (Bill) born to Jack & Betty on July 10th.

1937 Moved practice to The Ferns, 15 Laurel Grove, Penge. (Converts stable to a surgery.)

1939 Brings in Dr Davidson as a partner in the practice. (Davidson dies in the house.)

1940 Third child Robert, born to Jack & Betty on April 5th.

1940 Jack volunteers and joins the Royal Army Medical Corps (R.A.M.C.) on an emergency commission taking the rank of 2nd Lieutenant. Seconded to 5th Surrey Regiment stationed at Devonport.

1941 The Blitz on London. Jack moves the family to Cookham Dean, Berkshire.

Jack disembarks at Suez on 9th March. From there to Alexandria and on to a field hospital near Xania, Crete, arriving 19th April.

[For the chronology of Jack's movements throughout the War please see in the appendix the facsimile letter dated 31st October 1994 sent to Mrs S.Ruffle (née Readman) from the Ministry of Defence.]

May 1st. Start of aerial bombardment of Crete by the Luftwaffe.

Writes to Winifred, his sister, on 8th May (see appendix).

Writes to his brother-in-law, Claud, on 11th May (see appendix).

Writes to Betty on 12th May (see appendix).

May 20th. Airborne attack on Crete by German glider transport and parachute troops.

Jack becomes prisoner-of-war in Agia Roumeli on 1st June (see MOD letter to Mrs S. Ruffle).

1942   Fourth child Paul, born to Betty on July 21st.

1945   Fifth child Elizabeth, born to Betty on March 31st.

1946   Jack receives the MBE for 'gallant and distinguished service whilst prisoner of war'. (See appendix)

Sixth child, Susan, born to Jack & Betty on November 21st at Laurel Grove.

1972   While on a cruise to Australia, Jack dies on board the Ocean Monarch and is buried at sea off the Dutch Antilles.

1999   Betty dies aged 91.

During the writing of this novel, I spent many hours thinking about the character of John Readman (Jack) and his wife Elizabeth Readman (Betty). Both demonstrated love for each other and duty to others to a remarkable degree, despite the pressures that war heaped upon them. Each accepted the faults in each other, which may be incomprehensible to some who find infidelity inexcusable, even in some cases warranting an aggressive response.

I tried to deconstruct John's letter to his wife, which was written, under the stress of war, on their fourteenth anniversary. It is difficult to imagine the doctor sitting in his tent, dark except for the dim light of a hurricane lamp, composing lines which conveyed his emotions succinctly at a time of imminent bombardment.

What did he mean by 'I have hurt you lots and lots of times'? One has to enter the mind of a person in imminent danger who is writing what may be his final words. The 'hurts' may have been the normal disagreements married couples have in which something was said in anger. However John, in his earlier letter written on their tenth anniversary, admits to upsetting Betty in that he wrote: '...even if you can't love me in the way you used to do.' It seems that the relationship was not without the occasional blip.

Nevertheless, the facts speak for themselves. He returns from four years as a prisoner of war, during which time he has witnessed death and mutilation, to find that his family has increased by two children not of his seed; both bearing his surname.

Betty had borne the sacrifices which come with a man dedicated to his practice, Freemasonry, Rotary, the four-year absence of her husband and the 'hurts', whatever they were.

We shall never know if Betty harboured a grudge which weakened her resolve to be a faithful wife, as many wives succeeded in doing throughout the War. There is no evidence that she adopted a 'what's sauce for the gander is sauce for the goose' approach, if I may misquote an old saying. It is not intended that these facts should be weighed in scales of justice; just pointed up.

In Betty's case, there was the evidence of two babies in his absence by which she could be condemned. Much anguish must have been suffered by so many parties; Jack excessively so, Betty with her guilt of infidelity, the father of the two additional children losing a loving relationship with Betty and their children, the three elder boys missing their replacement father, and both sets of parents fretting for all concerned.

I write these lines merely to ponder the circumstances surrounding the lives of Jack and Betty; certainly not to be judgmental. It is sad to learn that Betty had many regrets and thought she had done some 'bad things', probably discounting the many good things she had done in her life.

I have concluded that Jack and Betty did succeed in being united in 'some sort of living progressive partnership', as Jack persuasively wrote to Betty. The couple accepted each other with all their respective failings. They were committed to 'see things through' for the sake of each other and their children.

Above all, it is forgiveness which emerges triumphant from the history of the Readmans. I see this as nothing short of admirable.

Graham Matthews

PREVIOUS PUBLICATIONS

'You're the *Doctor* - You Decide'
Growing up in the Blitz

Graham Matthews

ISBN 0-9547250-0-X
2004

'A Stone's Throw From Chancery Lane'

Graham Matthews

ISBN 0-9547250-1-8
2010